Young Writers 2005 CREATIVE WRITING
COMPETITION FOR SECONDARY SCHOOLS

T·A·L·E·S·

From Northern England
Edited by Lynsey Hawkins

 Young**Writers**

First published in Great Britain in 2005 by:
Young Writers
Remus House
Coltsfoot Drive
Peterborough
PE2 9JX
Telephone: 01733 890066
Website: www.youngwriters.co.uk

SB ISBN 1 84602 230 4

Foreword

Young Writers was established in 1991 and has been passionately devoted to the promotion of reading and writing in children and young adults ever since. The quest continues today. *Young Writers* remains as committed to engendering the fostering of burgeoning poetic and literary talent as ever.

This year, *Young Writers* are happy to present a dynamic and entertaining new selection of the best creative writing from a talented and diverse cross section of some of the most accomplished secondary school writers around. Entrants were presented with four inspirational and challenging themes.

'Myths And Legends' gave pupils the opportunity to adapt long-established tales from mythology (whether Greek, Roman, Arthurian or more conventional eg The Loch Ness Monster) to their own style.

'A Day In The Life Of ...' offered pupils the chance to depict twenty-four hours in the lives of literally anyone they could imagine. A hugely imaginative wealth of entries were received encompassing days in the lives of everyone from the top media celebrities to historical figures like Henry VIII or a typical soldier from the First World War.

Finally 'Short Stories', in contrast, offered no limit other than the author's own imagination while 'Hold The Front Page' provided the ideal opportunity to challenge the entrants' journalistic skills, asking them to provide a newspaper or magazine article on any subject of their choice.

T.A.L.E.S. From Northern England is ultimately a collection we feel sure you will love, featuring as it does the work of the best young authors writing today.

Contents

Shane Handley (12)	32
Jonathan Sykes (12)	33
Becky Howard (12)	34
Kieran Wilkinson (12)	35
Andrew Thompson (13)	36
Jessica Guy (12)	38
Justine Severs (13)	39
Emma Dawson (11)	40
Emma Bassett (12)	41
Lauren Watson (13)	42
Lauren Thomas (13)	43
Emily Saunders (12)	44
Joshua Harrison (12)	45
Daniel Phillips (11)	46
Alexandra Tombling (12)	47
Aaron Moon (12)	48
Wayne Smith (12)	49
Laura Hughes (12)	50
Daniel Redmond (11)	51
Bradley King (11)	52
Olivia Thompson (12)	53
Nicola Coates (12)	54
Kate Stephenson (12)	55
David Siddaway (13)	56
Callam Stevenson (13)	57
Natalie Cronin (13)	58
Tania Culley (13)	60
Benjamin Rutledge (13)	61
Launa McGlade (13)	62
Melissa Hugill (12)	63
Callie Jo Lowes (11)	64
Laura Henderson (11)	65
Amy-Louise Foulkes (12)	66
Jodi Turner (11)	67
Megan Dales (12)	68
Austin Sisson (12)	69

Lord Lawson of Beamish School, Birtley

Kate Pearson (12)	70
Lena Platow (12)	71
Karl Richardson (12)	72

Margaret Sutton School (Moderate Learning Difficulties), South Shields

Our Lady & St Bede RC School, Stockton-on-Tees

The Creative Writing

My Myth About The Sky

I suspect you were never told the truth about how the sky is blue. You see I've wondered why it isn't green, purple or black, well, let me tell you.

It all started thousands of years ago when the weather was terrible in Great Britain (a bit like it is today really). Billy Townsend was walking down the street - everyone darted inside! However, Billy stayed outside; all of a sudden the sky, which was green at that time, fell! It hit Billy on the head hard . . .

From that day everybody hated Billy. He became the man who'd made the sky fall. He had to do something, he had to make a new sky. So off Billy went. Firstly, he made a beautiful purple sky, but it got mixed up with the sea (you know that the sea is clear but it reflects the colour of the sky), so Billy painted it a lovely red, obviously it got confused with the sea too! So once again Billy painted the sky but he painted it yellow, only this time it got confused with the sea and sun! That was it! This time he would paint it for the last time, this time he would choose his favourite colour - blue. Off he went and painted it but this time it still got confused with the sea. He was so angry that he chucked white paint all over it; he turned away and everyone cheered. He looked back, the white bits of paint made the sea stand out from the sky!

Rachelle Falloon (11)
Bebside Middle School, Blyth

The Griffocilla's Last Song

What goes around the world but stays in a corner? Don't know, the answer? Well if you were asked this by a griffocilla, her song would haunt you for the rest of your 24-hour life.

A griffocilla is a ferocious beast: the wings of an eagle, a snake for a tail, a lioness' head, the hind quarters of a horse and three heads, and our heroine, Helena, the only one to survive the song.

Our story is set in Ancient Greece in the city of Atlantis. In the mountain pass, in the cave, lived the griffocilla. The griffocilla guarded the all-powerful, all healing, flower of Raneti. A man walking up the mountain was suddenly pounced on by the griffocilla,

'Answer, mortal, this riddle and you may have the fabled flower of Raneti. What's yellow, black and red all over?' asked the griffocilla.

'Ummm! It's a ... no, I give up,' said the man.

'Wrong, the answer is a tablet. Goodbye, mortal. My song is deadly. You got it wrong. This is my song - to get the flower you were my guest, you got it wrong, 24 hours you've got left.' At that, the griffocilla took flight, taking the mortal by the tunic in her mouth. She flew above the town and dropped him in a piece of hay. '24 hours,' cried the griffocilla as she went back to the mountain to guard the flower of Raneti.

24 hours later the man died. The word spread about that they were being punished by the gods and if they were asked a riddle they would die.

Helena was the beautiful tax collector's daughter. She had heard of the man's fate and she decided that she would stop the griffocilla so she walked up the mountain pass where she was pounced on by the griffocilla.

'Answer, mortal, and the fabled flower of Raneti is yours. What can you use all round the world yet will always come from Greece?' asked the griffocilla.

'Poor griffocilla,' Helena said with a smile, 'I'm a tax collector's daughter, therefore I know the answer is . . . Drachmas.'

'That's right, you win. Into my cave and there is the flower,' groaned the griffocilla.

So Helen entered the cave and there was the flower, glowing gold. She plucked the flower and left.

'You command me now, tell me what I must do,' said the griffocilla.

'You are a guardian and I have taken the thing you guarded. I want you to guard my city - the city of Atlantis. Guard us and protect us from the other civilisations,' requested Helena.

Helena scampered onto the griffocilla's back and they flew high in the sky.

Stephanie Ann Gallon (11)
Bebside Middle School, Blyth

Double Murder At Local School

A team of police officers are investigating a double murder at Blakeston Community School.

Last night caretaker, David Sutherland, found two bodies. The dead were named as Fred Thomson, a Blakeston pupil, and Stephen Wood, a teacher at the school.

Mr Sutherland told me he found the first body in the courtyard, police believe he was pushed through a second-storey window. The second body was found in a wood tech classroom. The police confirmed both bodies were found in suspicious circumstances. An electric saw was still running when Mr Wood's body was found.

Inspector Hall of Stockton's CID told me his officers now have the huge task of taking statements from staff and pupils at the school. Inspector Hall will be giving a press conference later on today.

The relatives of the two victims were too upset to talk to reporters. Mr Sutherland, the caretaker, has been offered counselling.

The head of Blakeston School, Mrs English, spoke of the devastating news. 'Mr Wood has been a teacher at the school for 13 years and was very safety conscious. The school has never experienced any serious accidents in this area'. She went on to say that the pupil, Fred Thomson, was a model pupil. 'He was involved in many of our after school clubs, especially the football team'.

Many of his classmates are traumatised by this terrible incident. Any pupil who feels they need counselling will be given it.

David Saddington (12)
Blakeston School, Stockton-on-Tees

Mr Henderson's Shed

Mr Henderson was my next-door neighbour. He had lived there for ten years. I longed to know what was in his shed and when he left his keys with my mum, (he was going on holiday), I knew this was my chance to explore the shed.

Later on that day, my mum went shopping. She left the keys but I didn't dare go in the shed. So I just forgot about them. Ten minutes later Mum came back. She made the tea and when it was done, she shouted me.

It was six o'clock. I shut all the curtains and put the lights on and I went out the back to the shed. I unlocked the shed door and opened it slowly. I was really scared. I saw a box; it wasn't just a normal box. It looked very different from all the other boxes there. I opened the box very slowly and it had …

My mum shouted to me to hurry up and I shouted, 'OK, be right there.'

I quickly looked in the box and I found some swords and other things but I didn't know what they were. Why were they there … ?

Jennifer Harland (13)
Blakeston School, Stockton-on-Tees

Mr Henderson's Shed

I longed to know what was in there and when he left his keys with my mam, (he was going on holiday), I knew this was my chance.

Later that night I walked out of my house and sneaked into next-door's garden and up to Mr Henderson's house. It was around midnight. I walked into the house and locked the front door. I had a torch with me so I didn't have to put the lights on. I walked into the kitchen and opened the back door. I snuck into the back garden so no one would see me.

By this time it was 1am. As I opened the shed door this horrid stench seeped out of the shed. I thought to myself, *what is making this horrid stench?* As I looked around I heard a bang. I wondered was it was. I looked around but there wasn't anything moving and nothing in the shed. I stepped into the shed wondering what to do next.

I looked in boxes to see what I could find. All of a sudden something flew down at me. I screamed but I suddenly stopped there and then before someone heard me.

I ran out and locked the shed door behind me, but as I was locking the door I looked around and I saw that a light was on in Mr Henderson's house! I had never turned a light on in there, I was scared! He must have come back!

Lucy Moran (13)
Blakeston School, Stockton-on-Tees

Mr Henderson's Shed

Mr Henderson was my next-door neighbour. He had lived there for ten years. We didn't know very much about him but were curious as to what was in his shed at the bottom of his garden. I longed to know what was in there and when he left his keys with my mam, (he was going on holiday), I knew this was my chance to explore the shed.

Later on in the day when Mr Henderson had left to go on holiday I said to my mam, 'Can I have the keys, Mam? I want to have a look at the keyring.' My mam gave me them. I snuck out the back whilst my mam was watching telly.

I quickly opened the shed and I couldn't believe what I saw - a tiny rocket ship! I climbed into it but I didn't know what to do next. Suddenly I knew, I pressed the green button and I heard a siren and there was a man shouting, '5, 4, 3, 3, 1, blast-off!' I was scared. I was thrown up in the air. I shattered the shed roof right open.

Once in the air I thought, *this is great!* I rode it like a jet. I went past a police car, they chased me. I could not go any faster! I felt as if it was going to blow up. There was no fuel left. I thought, *I want to go on this every day!*

All of a sudden I landed back in Mr Henderson's garden shed. 'Every day should be like this,' I laughed.

Nathan Pitt (13)
Blakeston School, Stockton-on-Tees

Mr Henderson's Shed

I longed to know what was in Mr Henderson's shed so when he left his keys with my mam, I made my way nervously to his garden. I opened the shed door and couldn't believe what I saw …

I saw a chair at first and then the rest. It was like a little house, it had a chair and a table and lots of trophies. I wanted to know what the trophies were for so I went in for a closer look. There were hundreds of them, he was obviously very good at school.

I looked closer and saw there was a huge trophy but not just any trophy. It was a trophy for being a very good runner. I loved sports. Then I heard a creaking noise. I didn't know where to look so I hid, but it was just Mr Henderson's cat called Whiskers.

Whiskers hissed at me. I thought my eyes were deceiving me as I thought I saw Mr Henderson and I did! He came over. I was scared at first but only at first as then he laughed at me and said, 'Come on, you'll be like me one day!'

I knew then that there was a long friendship ahead.

Chantelle Readman (13)
Blakeston School, Stockton-on-Tees

Mr Henderson's Shed

Mr Henderson was my next-door neighbour. He had lived there for ten years. We didn't know very much about him but were curious as to what was in his shed at the bottom of his garden. I longed to know what was in there and when he left his keys with my mam (he was going on holiday), I knew this was my chance to explore the shed.

It was a fine morning and the street was peaceful. My mam was cooking in the kitchen. When I went into the kitchen I saw some keys on the table. 'Mam, whose are those keys?' I asked, worried.

'Oh, they are just Mr Henderson's,' Mam explained.

Then all of a sudden my heart skipped a beat. As my mam went upstairs I grabbed the keys and ran to Mr Henderson's house. I went round the back and saw the shed at the bottom of the garden.

Now this Mr Henderson was a very poor man and he had no children or a wife so I didn't expect to find much.

I finally reached the shed and opened the door slowly. Then, all of a sudden, when I went inside I saw suitcases filled with money! I wondered why he had all that money there when he was poor. Anyway, it was very creepy.

Then I heard some footsteps coming towards the shed. I hid behind the workbench. The door opened and I think you know who it was - yes, it was Mr Henderson! I suddenly started shaking badly . . .

Jennifer Broadbent (12)
Blakeston School, Stockton-on-Tees

Granny Goes Back To Grass Roots!

When granny Pat Tabram bakes, neighbours often comment on the wonderful aromas that stray from her kitchen window. The 67-year-old has gladly shared recipes with most of her friends, but it is the most important ingredient that makes her cooking so sought after.

'Cannabis, a high-grade drug,' she reveals. 'Up until a year ago I had the worst back pain from a car accident. I was prescribed medication by my doctor but the side-effects were unbearable. Some days I'd lock myself away in a room and never want to come back out. Then my neighbours, who hadn't seen me out of the house for weeks, noticed so they came round and left me a couple of cigarettes. I smoked them and then slept for 12 hours which was the most I had slept for a long time. I woke up with an appetite for the first time in months as well. The next day I asked my friend what was in the cigarettes and they said that it was cannabis and I couldn't believe it!'

Pat had never tried any drugs before apart from those prescribed by her doctor. Through trial and error, Pat learnt how much cannabis to put in her cooking. She told us, 'I'm not a criminal, I'm self-medicating myself. I wish someone had told me years ago that being a 'criminal' would be this much fun!'

Natalie Dixon (11)
Blakeston School, Stockton-on-Tees

Michael Jackson Gunned Down

Last night Michael Jackson was gunned down by an unknown person. Mr Jackson was at his home in Never Land in California. The pop singer is critically ill in hospital. The police believe that the perpetrator was the father of one of the children who accused Mr Jackson of rape. The person was believed to be 5ft 6 and had a shaved head, he was wearing blue Nike tracksuit bottoms and had a blue and white Nike jacket to match.

Chief Inspector Joshua Smith said today, 'Michael's case is one of our top priorities as he is in intensive care and critically ill in hospital. If Michael Jackson dies then it will become a murder charge'.

Michael's charges for his child abuse case cannot go on any further until he is well enough or can pull through sufficiently to continue with his case.

If you have any information then please contact the police on 0800 6564633.

Lauren Smith (12)
Blakeston School, Stockton-on-Tees

Meg And The Drago

On a wonderful island called Greece the giant sun blazed down on the enormous patchwork fields and the tall oak trees bloomed on huge hills with streams flowing down. Sandy pebbled beaches ran for miles and the shimmering sun stretched further than the horizon.

Just as the people of Greece were enjoying the perfect weather, a huge cloud took over the sky. It began to rain red blood! The people of the town knew what this was ... the Drago had returned from the depths of Hell!

Off the coast of Greece was a smaller island called Crete which was ruled by a rich and wise king named Dieago. In his kingdom there were many servants but Dieago could only count on one, she was pretty and intelligent - Meg. Meg had brown hair which she always had clipped back with a slide she had received from her late grandma. Her eyes were oak-brown. Meg lived in a cottage behind the palace.

The next morning there was a knock on Meg's door; she opened the door and gasped, 'Oh, Your Majesty, I'm not late am I?'

'No, no, late last night I received a letter; it seems as though Queen Lola and her island are in terrible danger from the Drago,' the king replied.

'Oh no, that's terrible, can I do anything to help?' Meg asked in shock.

'As a matter of fact, yes, I'd love you to go and see Queen Lola and ask if you can help,' the king replied.

Meg quickly packed her bags and set off on her journey to Greece. It wasn't long before she arrived at the queen's palace. Meg was amazed at the beauty of the palace. She soon snapped out of her trance when the queen gasped, 'Meg darling, Dieago said you'd be here soon. Anyway I'll just run the mission by you and then you can decide, OK? My son Hercules has been captured by that terrible beast Drago. I need you to go and help him. I might not ever see him again,' Lola sobbed.

'Sure, I'll do it.' Meg replied.

'Splendid,' Lola said with a smile on her face. 'To help you on your way I have some equipment to protect you,' and Lola gave Meg a small bag. Inside the bag was an invisibility band to tie around her head and a wishing necklace. 'The wishes must come from your heart,' said Lola.

Meg battled scorching sunsets, blistering winds, dangerous mountains, all this to save the island of Greece. She soon reached the dark cave. She tiptoed to the entrance and carefully placed the band upon her head. Within seconds she disappeared. She walked through the cave some more when there, straight in front of her, chained to a wall was Hercules.

'Help,' Hercules cried. Hung upon the wall close to Hercules was a shiny key.

Meg went to grab the key when a voice bellowed, 'Your mother has sent no one and in three hours you will never see day again.'

'No!' Hercules screamed.

Meg turned her head and a mysterious figure turned in the shadows. *Was that the Drago?* Meg thought as she removed her headband and reappeared to the world. 'Shush,' Meg whispered, 'we don't want the Drago to return.'

'I wouldn't say that,' Hercules said.

Meg turned her head, staring at her was a long, scaled face, huge frightening teeth and breath like an ogre's foot. The Drago boxed them into a corner.

Was this the end for Meg and Hercules … ?

Lyndsey Cormack (12)
Blakeston School, Stockton-on-Tees

The UK's Strangest Bunny

On Wednesday 11th May 2005, a man sat down on a bench after having a lovely long walk in the park. Just then, out of the corner of his eye, he saw an amazing, colourful bunny, all covered in different-coloured spots. He couldn't believe his eyes, so he quickly got out his camera and started to take pictures of it.

At first the journalists just didn't believe him, they said that he was going mad in the head or something. But straightaway, they started to receive lots of pictures of the bunny, taken by various people. The journalists were confused and shocked so they decided to put up a sign saying … *The amazing colourful bunny! £100,000 reward for whoever captures the colourful bunny alive!*

Jennifer Berriman (12)
Blakeston School, Stockton-on-Tees

A Day In The Life Of Mary I

After saying goodbye to Mum, history lessons would never be boring again after what happened next …

The Tudors were my history subject that day. As usual, the teacher's droning voice was sending me to sleep, his last words I heard were, 'Mary I … '

Next thing I knew I was sitting on the throne wearing a crown and people were calling me 'Your Majesty'. Imagine me, Queen of England, having all the power of life and death of everyone in England!

One of my assistants gave me some letters to sign which I did without looking. I was getting bored so I wandered over to the window overlooking the courtyard. The day's executions had started; from the corner of my eye I noticed my best friend standing there with her hands tied. I thought, *this can't be right*. I rushed over to my desk and there, lying in front of me were the papers I'd signed - death warrants and on the bottom of the pile was her name. How could I have done this to her? I'd signed her death warrant without looking!

Thud, as the axe fell; my friend was next in line - I didn't want to be queen anymore. I had to stop this happening. I ran to the window shouting, *'Stop!'* but nobody heard me. As the axe went down, a ringing came to my ears.

I woke with a start and immediately gave my best mate a hug.

Next lesson, Joan of Arc could be interesting!

Sandy Harrison (12)
Blakeston School, Stockton-on-Tees

A Day In The Life Of A Victorian Girl

Another day! Woke up this morning at 6am to help my mum with the housework. There's a lot to be done. My dad can't help with it and Thomas has to clean chimneys today. My mum's not happy with him as he broke one of the windows with his football so he has to pay her back. No school for him!

Anyway, I went downstairs and found my mum cooking breakfast, bacon and egg, so I joined in. My dad came rushing down the stairs, late. He kissed me and Mum and then bolted out the door. That's his wages cut today. Thomas came down in his nightwear. Mum told him off so he want back upstairs, dressed and reluctantly came down, ate his breakfast then walked out to do his job.

Spring-clean day today so I cleaned out all the cupboards. Then Mum gave me a penny to go out with. I met Alison at the shop buying some toffees. I bought some as well, then we went down to the park to play skips. I won as usual! My balance was perfect.

Then I went home for a bath at 5.30pm before my brother got home. A lovely long bath in front of the fire. Next I put on my nightclothes and snuggled down in front of the fire to finish my knitting. I finally completed my rag doll and then I had to go to bed as I have the chance to go to school tomorrow. Can't wait.

Billie Mari Whitehead (12)
Blakeston School, Stockton-on-Tees

The Blakeston Times

Horror As Police Find Elvis Dead!

Last night police went to the home of singer, Elvis Presley, after his manager hadn't seen or talked to him in three days. The police had to break down the door to search the whole house; finally, as they went into the upstairs bathroom, they found him lying over the toilet seat.

Police reported that they think he may have taken an overdose as they found an empty bottle of anti-depressants on the floor in the bathroom.

A witness said that they saw an ambulance come round the corner and stop outside the star's house. They reported they rushed outside only to find a black body bag had been taken into the ambulance.

When the neighbour discovered who it was, they said that they had always liked the star and couldn't believe he was dead. Through a face of tears, they said that the last time they had spoken to the star they had had a row and felt terrible that the last time they saw each other they had parted on bad terms.

Detective Jackson reported that investigations were continuing and update would be given as soon as possible.

Jessica Binns (11)
Blakeston School, Stockton-on-Tees

Mr Henderson's Shed

'Mam, I'm home,' I shouted.

'How was school?' she asked.

'You know, the same as every other day,' I answered.

'OK, what are you going to do now?' she asked.

'I'm going to check on Mr Henderson's garden,' I replied.

'OK,' she replied.

So off I went to the shed. I put the key in the padlock and went to turn it when . . .

'Mark, Mark,' shouted my mam.

'Yes,' I replied.

'Tom's on the phone.'

'OK,' I replied.

I went into the house to get the phone.

'Hi Mark, are you coming out?' Tom asked.

'No, but you can come round here if you want and stay for tea.'

'OK, see you in five minutes,' he replied.

I waited for him to come round. When he arrived I told him I'd been hearing funny noises and my pets had been going missing. We went up to the shed, put the key in the lock when . . .

'Tom, Mark, tea,' shouted my mam.

'OK, coming,' I replied.

We went in for tea. 'That's the second time that's happened, we will try after our tea.'

After our tea we went down to the shed, put the key in the padlock, turned it, then the door opened. There, in cages, were my pets that had gone missing! He had been starving them. They were dead and had been stuffed. I ran off to tell my mam but she wouldn't believe us.

'Come and see for yourself!'

She did and she was amazed. She phoned the RSPCA and the police.

When Mr Henderson came back, he was arrested.

Ashley Wilsher (12)
Blakeston School, Stockton-on-Tees

Mr Henderson's Shed

On the afternoon of July 14th I was sitting in our family armchair waiting for Mr Henderson to arrive so that I could finally go onto his land. The doorbell rang at approximately 3.15pm that afternoon. When I heard it I leapt out of the armchair and lunged for the door.

'Hello, Billy, how are you today?' Mr Henderson asked.

'I'm great, thank you for asking,' I replied. I was wetting myself with excitement. I just couldn't wait for him to leave.

After a few minutes of talking, Mr Henderson finally drove off. After shutting the door, I walked into the kitchen because I wanted to make sure I was allowed to go. I looked in the kitchen and nobody was there so I went anyway, although I hadn't been given permission. When I reached the door, my mam reached the top of the stairs and spotted me walking out of the door.

'Billy, where do you think you're going?' my mam screamed at the top of her voice.

'Out,' I replied to her.

'No, you're not!' my mam yelled.

Because of being grounded, I wasn't allowed out so I had my supper and watched telly. By that time it was 11.04pm so I got changed and went to sleep.

The next morning I got up really early to go out for my daily run via Mr Henderson's house. I sneaked down the stairs as quietly as possible. My mam was already downstairs getting ready for work but fortunately she didn't hear me. When she walked out of the door, I snatched the keys quickly but quietly and walked out.

After she'd locked the door I jumped over Mr Henderson's fence and into his back garden. I was shaking like a baby's rattle. Finally I found the nerve and unlocked the shed door. I couldn't believe my eyes as I went in! The stench of dead corpses and the sight of guns, ammo and the interrogation chair.

I locked up the shed and ran, I was running as fast as a cheetah until I got to the park, I couldn't believe my next-door neighbour was a murderer!

David Charlton (12)
Blakeston School, Stockton-on-Tees

House

If the villagers knew what was happening, they'd be screaming and running away terrified.

Mist rolled in thick and fast, soon engulfing their little village. Drops of water on the cobblestones turned to puddles - the moisture clinging to everything, forcing its way into the smallest cracks.

Hope, a seven-year-old girl, stirred inside her wooden house; she crept down the stairs trying not to disturb her father. From the effort of being so quiet, Hope failed to realise the walls of her house were wringing wet, although she did realise the paddling pool she was standing in at the bottom of the stairs; the whole floor was glazed with water. The next thing she did was natural, she screamed!

Her father, a burly man, came bounding down the stairs intending to comfort his daughter until he saw the house - flashes of terror blazed from his eyes and shone across Hope's.

A deafening crack broke the silence; Hope was terrified, now crying. 'Daddy!'

'Hope, we have to get out … now!' came the reply.

'Daddy, what's wrong?' Hope's voice trembled as she was being pulled along by her father's firm grip.

'The houses are collapsing, the weight of the water is pulling them down, it's just too much!' he cried.

Houses were dropping quickly, a painful ringing entered Hope's ears but she saw her back door; they were out, the mist whipping their faces.

Hope looked back as a fresh wave of tears hit her, 'Daddy, the village has gone!'

Lisa Richardson (12)
Bydales School, Redcar

A Day In The Life Of The Number One Spy

They were gaining fast on her. She came to the edge of the cliff of death. She had to make a decision; if she liked it or not, the life of death decision! She looked down the long, sharp, scary, dangerous cliff. She looked back; all the soldiers formed a straight line in front of her. She took another look down the cliff, then she turned, unzipped her long, black, warm coat, took a deep breath. She saluted and jumped backwards. She plummeted straight towards the water.

A rope was hurled to her. She grabbed hold of it and she was raised into the sky. It was the Grand Turk. As she came aboard, all the men were staring with their jaws wide open like a lion ready to pounce.

The captain waltzed straight up to her and whispered, 'What would you have done if we weren't here?'

Before he could say anything else she replied, 'Well, I would have gone to plan B but don't ask what that is because I always make it up as I go along.'

Out of nowhere, there were about a million shots fired at the ship. One hit the captain and unfortunately killed him. He soon went cold like the North Pole but he was able to whisper, 'You're in charge.' She felt very uncomfortable as she was the only woman or 'spy' onboard.

As the ship got underway another million shots were fired. The top sail slammed to the deck …

Claire Jackson (14)
Bydales School, Redcar

Road To Hell!

Michael Greening, the man accused of a series of sex attacks on girls and women between the ages of 10 and 52 in and around London's M25 area, wept as he told police: 'I've been gay most of my life'.

He denies all charges while DNA traces have provided the billion-to-one evidence against him. Michael insists he was only interested in men and spent his nights cruising gay haunts. 'I would go and meet people. It was pretty stupid like, but I've already told you I am gay, so I was meeting men, for the usual gay things'.

Mrs Greening, weeping and covering her face with her hands, told the court she had found condoms in his pocket.

Michael Green is in custody at the South London jail for the related charges surrounding this investigation, rape, burglary and sodomy, that are considered measure eleven offences. The City's email system is not functioning this weekend.

A mug photo is available at the South Station. Detective, Jim Strovink will be available at the South Station for additional information and interviews. The detective told the news, 'This is the biggest case of my career and I would like to be kept in the loop'.

Daryl Wheatley (14)
Dene Community School of Technology, Peterlee

UFO Hits America

A Miss Alex Smith witnessed the amazing sight; on her way home from her night job at the 24-hour café on Linken Road in New York. She looked up and an object was coming down with incredible speed. The round object had orange neon lights on the bottom and was made out of some sort of aluminium.

At the moment the aircraft is in a medical lock-up and the creatures are in the Medical Science lab.

The scientist involved claims it could uncover something superior to humans.

Rhys Carr (13)
Dene Community School of Technology, Peterlee

Murder In The ABC Park!

A brutal murder has taken place in the ABC park at Horden. The victim, a girl aged sixteen, was later identified as Louise Harper, her body was found by street warden, Frank Scott.

Frank found the girl in the ABC park and notified the police at once. The police did a full search of the park and found the girl's bag which helped them identify her as Louise Harper.

The bag contained the girl's mobile phone and broken bits of glass with her blood on. Her parents were notified immediately and were interviewed to see if they knew anything that might help with their investigation.

Police Officer Lee Mark had this to say, 'We urge anyone with information to come forward, if anyone saw anything strange, please notify the police'.

He also told us that Louise may have died in a lot of pain given that they think she was beaten to death. Police also suggested that young women should be careful, however, they do not think there is anything to worry about as they think the person concerned may have already left the area.

The police have already got a suspect and have begun searching for him. His name is Ian Carter; if you know where this man is, please contact the police and do not confront him as he may be dangerous.

Full story, pages 12 and 13.

Amy Dobson (14), Jodie Edwards & Stephanie Hughes
Dene Community School of Technology, Peterlee

Attack In The Underground

On Friday 13th May 2005, Iraqi terrorists planned to attack the London Underground's Waterloo tube station.

The tube station was in great danger of being flooded due to the terrorists planning to use a fifty-pound Semtex incendiary device.

Passengers who were ready to commute home, fled in terror as quickly as they could from the underground.

Security guards contacted the Metropolitan police for back-up and fortunately the Bomb Squad arrived in time to disarm what they said was a rather crude device.

'Fortunately, our trained staff reacted quickly and averted any deaths or injury of any kind. Also, if this bomb had exploded it would have caused major damage, even flooding of the line. Disruption would have been inevitable and may have run into months,' said Mr James Donaldson, head of underground security.

Kimberley Russell (14) & Mariel Jones
Dene Community School of Technology, Peterlee

The Tornado

On a bright, lovely Bank Holiday Monday, everybody was on their way to get their pay.....(?) when a man saw something in the distance. When it started to get closer, the man realised it was a tornado so he immediately informed the village.

When the tornado hit the village it caused a disaster. Over 20 people died in the tornado. It took four weeks to get everything back up and running.

When everything was back to normal, everyone congratulated the man for saving people's lives. Had it not been for him they would all have died.

The Queen was so proud of this man that she sent him a telegram and gave him a knighthood.

He was also very proud of himself!

Tony Hogwood (13)
Dene Community School of Technology, Peterlee

The Empire

Our tale begins with a kingdom called Sivloat. The Baron of Sivloat and his son rule Sivloat, but the empire ruled by the corrupt patriot who's evil and twisted and his henchman, Magi Magmas, have hated Sivloat for years, they are one step away from crushing it. Those who attack him or deny his leadership change their minds overnight, or are killed for betrayal. People live in fear, no one can escape the empire.

Snow has hit Sivloat early and Artos (the baron's son) rides to see his father.

'I have a task for you … ' states his father, 'gather the harvest to prove you're worthy of taking over.'

So Artos gathers some of his father's men and rides to the farms. When they reach the first farm, it is burning. Then outlaws rush in, Artos sees them and quickly orders his men to form up; they charge at them and hack them down, it is over in seconds.

Suddenly, the sky goes black. The empire emerges from the valley, the baron shouts, 'Stand aside Artos, I shall deal with this.'

The Sivloat army forms outside the town. The empire's troops march forward past the farm and form on a field right next to the city. The evil Bishop Lothal marches forward with some troops and the Baron of Sivloat steps forward.

'Get off my lands!' states the baron.

'You have been accused of slavery and your lands and title are done for.'

'Liar, there are no slaves here!' Then he receives a blow to the head and he drops.

'Crush the city.'

The Bishop Lothal walks away. Sivloat is in flames in seconds. Artos grabs his sword and slits his own throat. Sivloat is doomed.

Jeff Mawhinney (12)
Dene Community School of Technology, Peterlee

Ferret's Diary Entry

Hello, my name is Ferret. I have just come back to school. I was very worried and very scared because I had met some horrible people, at school, they had been very nasty. I felt very worried when I was told I was going to school in case I got hit by all the nasty people who were there.

My class was 4F and I had all the nasty people in my class, but the teacher was very nice because she gave me sweets and stickers, but everyone took the mick out of me. That was the bad thing about this school. They were all nasty and would hang around in big gangs while I just sat in the corner on a bench and they would all shout, 'No mates?' to me. If I told the teacher they would all gang up on me.

The next day when I went to school I met a boy called Beany. His mam asked me if I wanted to go for a drive in her car but I said, 'No.' but I'd still met a nice new friend called Beany.

I was very disappointed because my school is good but the people in the school are naughty.

Anthony Caley (12)
Eston Park School, Middlesbrough

A Day In The Life Of A Vampire

Hi, my name's Vicky. If you haven't guessed, I'm a vampire, and I'm telling you about an ordinary day to me.

I have to be careful I don't die, so on a morning I'm really busy. Yeah, I know what you're thinking, *but doesn't she sleep in the morning?* Not this vampire! I'm not letting sunlight stop me. Here's what I do every morning.

When I wake up I make my coffin. After I've had blood flakes and blood for breakfast, I clean my fangs and sharpen them with a fang file. I dress in my black robe and then make sure all of my body is covered in Factor 100 suncream (vampire special, you'll never see that in the shops!). By the way, I always make sure I am wearing my silver bullet, lead and wooden stake-proof jacket, and have my anti-crucifix spray. Then I put on my silver bullet detector, a bat bracelet with eyes that flash in the presence of a silver bullet. Finally, I make sure I look gruesome and powder my face white and make my lips redder with lipstick. Now I'm ready to start the rest of the day.

Firstly, I absolutely love flying. I spend most days flying around, looking for something to eat. When I do go out I have to go on breaks to reapply my suncream. Then at night I go back to my castle and sleep in my comfortable coffin.

I'm a 'one of a kind' vampire!

Lisa McGrath (12)
Eston Park School, Middlesbrough

The Old Park

'Sophie, get down here now and do these dishes, I won't ask you again!' shouted Jane, whilst struggling to feed her two-year-old son Tom.

'Mum, I've told you, I'm going out!' Sophie replied, getting ready.

Sophie came downstairs fussing in the mirror with her long brown hair.

'Don't go near that old park, you never know who's there!' said her mum, shuddering at the thought.

'OK,' sighed Sophie.

'You coming to the Old Park, Soph?' asked Vicki when they were out.

'I can't, er, I don't want to!' But in the end Sophie said, 'Yeah, let's go. Mum won't find out.'

When they got there Sophie noticed a group of older lads that she had never seen before.

'Don't worry!' reassured Vicki. So they went to join the rest of their mates.

They were all having a great time until Rachel and Gemma, two other friends of Sophie, brought two bottles of wine.

'Oh! I don't think so!' exclaimed Sophie. '*Drink* at our age? We're only 13!'

Later on, Sophie and her other friends were drunk when some lads came over and started saying things to them. Suddenly, out of the blue, an older lad leaned over Sophie to kiss her but fiercely she pushed him away.

Luckily, as she was driving past, Sophie's mum picked them up and told the boys to stay away. Sophie and her friends never went back!

Victoria Cooper (11)
Eston Park School, Middlesbrough

A Day In The Life Of A World War II Nurse

Hello, my name is Fiona. I am eighty-three years old. I was a nurse in World War II. I have one daughter and two sons. Only my daughter was born during the war. She is sixty-four now. I will now tell you a bit of my life during the time of the disaster that was the war ...

I was eighteen when it all happened. A private nurse. A bomb hit Scotland while I was there. The Anderson shelters weren't that useful. Kids dying, blood all around. Everything was wrong. Five thousand soldiers were at war. How many would survive?

I went to the hospital where there were soldiers whose legs had been blown off. There wasn't much of a life in those days.

Our food was rationed, *no sugar, no milk.* My mother and father tried to support me but I still couldn't understand why it all had happened because my one-year-old son had died!

A nuclear bomb had gone off and my son was infected. His lungs corroded. Even now I cry, thinking how it happened to him. Why couldn't it have happened to me instead? How could anyone take him away? How would I survive without him?

The hospitals were packed. Soldiers dying. Needles on the side. The world was in chaos but I was in love. A young soldier, twenty years old; every time I saw him it sent a shiver up my spine. He made me happy. He was still alive, he was going to be mine!

I stitched up his wound and our eyes met!

Robyn Leigh McConnell (12)
Eston Park School, Middlesbrough

Bad Grannies

Once upon a time there lived two old aged pensioners who lived in an old folks' home. They both took three tablets a day to keep them calm, until one day they flushed their tablets down the toilet.

After a while, around dinner time, they started to go crazy and throw food about. Then suddenly they dived onto their electric wheelchairs and out of the doors they flew.

Out of the blue, in a motor shop, two grannies burst through the doors. They raced up and down the shop and soon found what they were looking for … a new motor for electric wheelchairs to make them go faster! They picked out the motors and fixed them onto their wheelchairs and sped off!

Later that day on the news, the two old pensioners nicknamed 'Bad Grannies' were seen looting in a supermarket. Twelve cops arrested them but they were fought them off with walking sticks.

Suddenly their wheelchairs blew up and they ran off, but after a wild goose chase in the shop, the grannies fell over some footballs.

The next day the grannies were sentenced to ten years in an old folks' home (if they lived that long!).

'Do you have anything to say?' asked the judge

And the grannies sang, 'Bad grannies,
Bad grannies,
What ya gonna do?
What ya gonna do when we loot off you?
We loot together,
We die together,
Bad grannies for life!'

Shane Handley (12)
Eston Park School, Middlesbrough

Alien Invasion

It was a normal Sunday morning on California beach. The sun was blazing, the skies were blue, but this was not any Sunday morning, this was Hallowe'en Sunday morning and all the children were getting their costumes out for the night.

But on planet Yougoplatainium (where aliens live), they were planning to come down to conquer Earth and immortalise all humans. However Mark Thomson and Wayne Doogle were SGIAB agents (Super Good Intelligent Alien Blasters) and were ready for any alien that landed on planet Earth.

A little boy called Timmy was on an aeroplane going to California beach airport and saw the black hole forming to let through the aliens from Yougoplatainium, but Timmy was the only person who could see the black hole because he had a special ability to see them.

Anyway, it was night and all the kids were out trick or treating in their costumes but the aliens were starting to come out of the black hole.

Boom, boom! A deep noise, and then smoke came from the door of an alien spaceship and two hundred and fifty aliens swarmed out of it.

Within 15 minutes of the aliens landing, California beach was more like Fire City but up pulled Mark and Wayne, the alien blasters in their alien blasting machine. 'I knew this would come in handy,' said Wayne.

'Let's get blasting,' said Mark. *Bang!* One of the alien's heads flew through the air and landed on the floor! 'Strike one,' said Mark.

Mark and Wayne blasted all the aliens and alien ships until all alien life forms and things were completely gone and California beach was safe.

As for Timmy, the alien blasters found out about his special ability and hired him to scout the airs for other warps.

Jonathan Sykes (12)
Eston Park School, Middlesbrough

Life Of Hell

He woke up into another day of hell. Day after day his life got worse. All the people around him made him feel unwanted, as if he wasn't there.

Chris climbed out of his bed and wandered downstairs into the kitchen where he saw his mum. He asked her if they were going out today but, same as usual, he was ignored.

His family was nasty to him, kids were ignorant and abusive to him, even his teachers never asked him for answers when he raised his hand.

Every night he wondered what it would be like if he were dead. In other words, commit suicide. He would lie on his bed and let his imagination run loose. Images would come up in his mind of him putting a knife to his heart or of him lying on the kitchen floor with blood all over. He always opened his eyes quickly as they were flooded with tears from the horrific flashes.

Time ticked by until it got to 3am. Chris was waiting until everyone went to bed, waiting so that when they did, he could creep downstairs and into the kitchen.

As he turned the kitchen handle slowly and opened the door, he forgot about his dog, Scamp, until Scamp came charging at Chris. Chris picked up Scamp and put him in the living room. He then went back into the kitchen and carefully shut the door. He opened a drawer and then took out the sharpest knife and shut the drawer. Chris then aimed the knife towards his stomach, shut his eyes and thrust the knife into his organ. *Thud … !*

Becky Howard (12)
Eston Park School, Middlesbrough

A Day In The Life Of Dracula

Now I know my life isn't very interesting but I want to bore you to death so I can drink your blood! My day usually starts with me having to wake up to a lifeless castle in my chamber. Then I refresh myself with a glass of freshly squeezed blood imported all the way from Brazil! After that I get dressed in my usual black and red garments.

By now I normally get a little peckish so I fly to Shaloanga for my daily feast of *blood!*

By now it's around six so I switch on my 56" TV and watch my favourite programme in the world, 'The Simpsons'. After 'The Simpsons' I get ready for bed and go to sleep. Well, dead yet? No? Well I'll have to come for you myself … *Ha, ha, ha, haaaa!*

Kieran Wilkinson (12)
Eston Park School, Middlesbrough

The Journey To Save Morgan-Le-Fait

Once upon a time there was a brave band of young and chivalrous knights. They had a quest. They had to save the fair maiden, Morgan-Le-Fait from the hero-slaying, all-feared dragon, the 500-year-old Drano, who had kept the damsel there for many a year, but the courageous knights were destined to save her.

The knights were called, Lombardo VIII (the leader), Leon Leonceour, Valten of Sigmar and Imerick of Ulthran (his fellow grail knights) and so they set out to save the damsel.

As they left the castle, they wandered down a long and winding path towards the land of the dead. They could smell the decomposing corpses from miles away. As they entered the forest, Imerick felt uneasy. All of a sudden, a half dead werewolf pounced on him and knocked him from his horse. Valten, fearing for his friend's life, struck the werewolf down to the ground. Imerick rose to his feet and, with a mighty blow, he impaled the werewolf with his deadly spear straight through his undead heart. The werewolf would not rise again. Imerick climbed back onto his horse and they all soldiered on.

Still in the undead land, they came upon a swamp. The odour reeked from every inch of slimy green mud. They dismounted from their horses in disgust as they could not travel over this mass of bogland. They began to wade their way through the huge amounts of marshland.

They made it out of the marshes and continued, slightly shaken but with no serious injuries. They carried on towards the dragon's keep and all four grail knights were still determined to save the damsel in much distress. They saw before them, after a long trek, a huge crater carved into the earth as if it were done by a dessert spoon of the gods. And in this crater, which they had to cross so as not to add days to Morgan-Le-Fait's suffering, there were horrors beyond any man or beast's worst nightmare. These went by the name of Garricks; the most terrible features about these animals were not their vicious and terrible teeth, nor their flesh-ripping claws but their terrible deadly way of killing their challengers. They would take out and reinstate their internal essential organs repeatedly so anyone who was caught by these repulsive creatures was not in for death but would be tortured eternally; death would be a blessing!

So they plucked up courage and walked towards 'the valley of the forever living'. As they scrambled down the slippery slope, Lombard VIII led the brave troops, after overcoming the werewolf in the marsh they still weren't calm. They would meet their end in this valley and they knew it.

The Garricks peered around every corner, they all wanted human flesh for dinner! One leapt onto Imerick, he was struck to the floor with a set of huge claws at his throat. Valten drew his huge long sword and struck the back of the beast. Its leathery hide deflected the blow with ease. Could nothing kill these ferocious beasts? Lombardo drew his bow and aimed a shot straight down the Garrick's throat. This did slay the beast but before the men could run away, the horrors were upon them, except this time there was more than one.

They were all to suffer everlasting heart-wrenching pain at the hands of those most experienced of torturers!

Andrew Thompson (13)
Eston Park School, Middlesbrough

The Goddess Of Love And Beauty

Once, before people of our time knew, there was a goddess of love and beauty. She was name Jessiciam and she had sea-blue eyes and beautiful blonde hair.

There were other goddesses but none as beautiful as her. Although another goddess who was not far off was the goddess of *envy* named Venus - she had long brown hair and emerald-green eyes. She became green with envy and decided to take drastic measures.

So after a while of thinking, she put a knife through Jessiciam's heart and when Jessiciam died, so did love and beauty which is the reason why some people have love affairs.

Because gods and goddesses can't be killed or destroyed by a mortal, only by another god or goddess, Venus had more power than any other.

Some time later, after Venus had become too powerful, all the gods and goddesses united to defeat Venus. They locked her up in a mountain. Frequently Jessiciam sent Venus visions of what a terrible goddess of love and beauty she was, from the place of the dead.

As Venus got frustrated trying to escape she banged on the walls of the mountain around her which caused earthquakes and shivers.

And now, our true goddess of love and beauty can rest in peace now that the truth has been told!

Jessica Guy (12)
Eston Park School, Middlesbrough

Guinevere Cheats on Arthur - With Camelot's Sir Lancelot

Guinevere has revealed to a hurt King Arthur that she has fallen in love with his best friend (talk about loyal!), Camelot's Sir Lancelot (sorry ladies).

This happened yesterday whilst they were having a quiet night in for his birthday (now he can say why he didn't like turning 40!).

Since this disturbing and gossipy news has come out into the open, King Arthur has now exiled Lancelot from the Round Table and told him to go away for a while.

Guinevere has moved out of the castle watched by the careful eye of King Arthur from their bedroom window.

They are taking each other to court to get custody of their three corgies, Humfred, Sassy and Betty. Guinevere should get the corgies as she was the one who adopted them, but Arthur says he is the one who has looked after them most and says he loves them more than anybody (more than her now).

The servants are deeply worried about Arthur as he hasn't come out of his room; he won't eat anything and he is making himself sick all the time.

We caught up with the king's mother, Andrea, to see what she had to say. She said, 'How can she do this? All he has done is love her and this is what she gives him in return'.

We can only wonder why Guinevere gave up diamonds and pearls for well ... Lancelot? What has he got that Arthur hasn't? (Arthur's only the King of England!)

Let's hope our king has a better birthday next year.

Justine Severs (13)
Eston Park School, Middlesbrough

Rapunzel

(The modern version)

Rapunzel was really enjoying her life. She got good grades in her GCSEs, lived with her family and friends, and her eighteenth birthday was in two days. The only problem was, her hair was really long, and I mean, really long! It was down to the floor and she couldn't get a hairdressing appointment.

The next day Rapunzel went shopping, but when she'd got everything, she realised she had no money to pay, so she legged it! Later on that day, the police caught her and locked her in a tower.

Weeks later, a man was passing by and saw her looking out the window. 'What ya doin' up there?' he asked.

So she told him her hair story. Five minutes later he suggested climbing up her hair and she agreed. But when he got up there, he said, 'And how do we get down?'

'There are some harnesses in that box over there,' Rapunzel replied.

'Well, why didn't you use them before?' he asked.

'Because I didn't know how to,' she replied.

Luckily he did, so they managed to get out of the tower. Once they were out, they arranged a flight to Spain and lived happily ever after - at least for a year or two!

Emma Dawson (11)
Eston Park School, Middlesbrough

The Lady Of Shalott

The lady who lives in a tower alone,
Never sees anything but her own home.
She weaves a picture of the world she never sees,
Of things like people, animals and trees.

She cannot look directly out of the window,
Instead looks in a mirror and sees the world as nothing
But shadow,
One day is all she asks to see more than just a room,
To talk, to run or just to look outside and see the moon.

She decides to go to Camelot,
To see the gorgeous Sir Lancelot.
Even though it will mean her death,
She knows she must, so she takes one last deep breath.

She feels her life slowly drain from her,
So she gets in a boat and leaves the world behind her.
As she floats down to Camelot, she slowly dies with grace,
And when she arrives, Sir Lancelot looks at her and says,
'She has a lovely face.'

And with that, the Lady of Shalott is no more.

Emma Bassett (12)
Eston Park School, Middlesbrough

Story Based On The Lady Of Shalott

Through her bedroom window, Jasmine watched the river flowing along, with lots of pretty daffodils and daisies on its riverbanks. It was a lovely sunny day outside and Jasmine was painting a detailed picture of the wonderful scenery surrounding her humble bungalow. Jasmine was a very talented artist, who was especially good at painting landscapes, but she had one problem to stop her from doing what she loved best - an allergy. Jasmine had a very unusual allergy to fresh air. Because of this she couldn't paint any real landscapes other than what she could see from her home.

Before she discovered her allergy, Jasmine used to be a very keen sportsperson. She loved being outside, and was always taking part in sports competitions. As she was tall and slim, with big blue eyes, pink lips and rosy cheeks, she was also a model for the children's section in catalogues. She had a huge interest in art and fashion, so took up drawing as a hobby.

It wasn't until Jasmine was fourteen that she had a fit while playing outside on a very hot day. She was kept in hospital for six months on a ventilator until the doctors figured out what was wrong with her. There wasn't much hope for Jasmine to survive, but she did.

One day Jasmine was looking out of her window through her beautiful, big, blue eyes, when she saw a group of celebrities walking past. This wasn't unusual, considering she lived in Hollywood, USA. As she looked closer, she noticed that, along with Johnny Depp and Ian McKellen, was Orlando Bloom. Jasmine had a huge crush on him, so even though it would risk her life, she knew she had to go out to get his autograph.

Jasmine rushed to her wardrobe. Putting on a white DKNY gypsy skirt with a pink vest top and white bolero jacket, with a big floppy sunhat and FCUK sunglasses, she ran outside and into a nearby taxi. She followed Orlando to 'The Ivy', a famous outside restaurant, and found herself a table. Rushing to where Orlando was sitting, she collapsed in the middle of the floor. He ran over to where Jasmine was lying and tried to resuscitate her, but it was too late. As he watched paramedics take her body away, he said lovingly, 'She has a beautiful face.'

Lauren Watson (13)
Eston Park School, Middlesbrough

King Arthur And The Knights
Of The Round Table.

Arthur was furious. His face was as red as a newly-inflicted wound. If he were a warhorse, his ears would be pricked and ready for the bugle to signal battle. His long jet-black hair swayed from side to side as the wind tried to escape as far away from him as possible. He watched like an assassin with the eagle's pinpoint eyes. He watched Sir Lancelot with his shining grey armour and luscious face. His horse gave away his position, for it was mysteriously black and always with Lancelot.

Lancelot had betrayed his king and stolen his everlasting love, Guinevere. The king had only been married for about thirteen months and now he was outraged at what he was seeing. Lancelot and Guinevere in love! There was a moment of freedom but the cold air swept reality back into his memory.

For the next few days he watched and watched, there was no time to waste, being rich he couldn't live without his love, but he thought neither could Lancelot and Guinevere.

The gossip was now all over the village of Camelot. People could not stop talking about it. The king was even more outraged! He couldn't even go into town for a ride without people either willing to blood-hunt Lancelot or people saying they felt very sorry for him. But people who had never experienced this form of anger and betrayal would never understand.

Throughout the next three weeks, he didn't talk to Guinevere, but never took his eye off her. Whenever the conversation came up of affair, Arthur either left the room or did something to occupy him until the conversation had ended.

After a few weeks he decided things had gone on long enough. He decided to speak up. 'Lancelot!' he screamed with such anger that I think the whole of Camelot came to a halt. Lancelot looked with fear and guilt in his eyes. 'You are exiled from these streets until I have forgiven you and I wouldn't blame myself if I never let you return. But we will never have the same relationship as we did before.'

Lancelot was then exiled for three years and was sentenced back only for war, but Arthur was right, the two of them never talked or looked at each other the same way.

Lauren Thomas (13)
Eston Park School, Middlesbrough

The Death Of Ann-Marie Magson

On Tuesday night at 11.20pm, Ann-Marie Magson's doorbell rang. Ann-Marie walked slowly to the door. She undid the lock and opened the door. A man barged through like a herd of elephants running for their lives. She tried to stop the man but he pushed her to the floor. Ann-Marie fell to the ground with a thud. She saw the man get hold of her very expensive vase, then the man got hold of her head and smashed it against the vase!

At this point Ann-Marie's daughter, Sarah, was round the corner from her mother's home. When Sarah finally got to her mother's she found her with her head pouring with blood. What was worse, her mother was tied to a chair with rope which was cutting into her wrists. Sarah quickly phoned the police and rang for an ambulance.

The ambulance got to Ann-Marie's house at 11.35pm. The ambulance took Ann-Marie to James Cook Hospital where she was put on a ventilator to try and keep her alive. But at 9.45am the doctors had given up. They switched the ventilator off. Ann-Marie Magson had died at the age of 79 years.

If anyone has any information on this crime, please contact the local police.

Emily Saunders (12)
Eston Park School, Middlesbrough

The Enlarging Machine

The legend began thousands of years ago in the year 2005.

Two friends, Nathan and Stewart, were around the Popeye Club with classmates from school. They were bragging about a machine they'd made in science; they named it 'the enlarging machine'.

At the weekend, Josh, Gus and Jess all went and followed the two friends down to the beach. Gus and his friends saw Stewart and Nathan going into an abandoned castle where rumour had it, some bloke had murdered his wife and strung himself up.

Josh, Gus and Jess lost sight of Stewart and Nathan, then out of the shadows they saw the bricks of the castle start to shake and pop out; it was obvious what had happened.

In a split second Nathan and Stewart emerged from the castle remains, their heads almost touching the clouds!

For the next few days, the world seemed to stand still as Nathan and Stewart made the world to their satisfaction. Nathan and Stewart ripped up buildings and chewed up cars.

The enlarging machine was in the remains of the rubble. They found the machine and shrank their bodies and Nathan and Stewart were small again.

Joshua Harrison (12)
Eston Park School, Middlesbrough

A Day In The Life Of A Dog

Today I was playing with my chew bone when I heard my owner say to this other man, 'Are you entering your Bully for the race?' he whispered. The race was not for two days. Then I ran out of the dog flap in the door to ask Bully if he was racing. He was!

The next day was the day before the race. I was practising with my owner for it. I was jumping over hurdles which my owner had borrowed from the gym. Then I went in my basket to have a nap.

I woke up and it was morning and because my owner was still in bed, I woke him up. 'OK, Daniel, let's go to the race, I'll get ready . . .'

I'm on the starting line, I have to go when the gun fires. It's gone! I'm second and Bully is first. Oh no! Bully has fallenl over right on the finish line so I've won!

After the race Bully was limping a bit but he told me that he was OK.

Daniel Phillips (11)
Eston Park School, Middlesbrough

A Day In The Life Of Monica Bing
From 'Friends'

Monica lives in Greenwich Village in New York. She has some very close friends, Rachel, Phoebe, Joey, Ross, her brother, and Chandler Bing, her husband. Monica works as a chef at a big New York restaurant.

In the morning she cooks breakfast for Chandler and hangs around with her friends. Then she sets off for work. When she is at work she serves delicious meals which all her customers, friends and family love. During the long day at work, for her dinner break she either goes home and has a little snack or she just has one at work.

In the evening when Monica arrives home from work, she hangs her coat up and prepares a tasty meal for Chandler and herself for when he gets home from work.

After tea, Monica hangs around with her friends at the coffee house (Central Perk) or at her apartment, then she goes to bed.

On Monica's day off she loves cleaning and is very fanatical about everything and where it is supposed to go. If her apartment is already clean, she goes to her friend Joey's apartment across the hall or to the coffee house again.

Alexandra Tombling (12)
Eston Park School, Middlesbrough

Freaky Friday

'Aaron! Wake up, we're going to your uncle's, it's his birthday.'

I stumbled out of my bed and while I was brushing my teeth I thought to myself, *the summer holidays are meant to be fun.* Soon enough I got ready and picked up my dog, Tyra, and set off to my uncle's. I was thinking of all the mischief Tyra and I could get up to.

Soon enough we got there, Tyra and I went to play 'fetch the ball' in his house. Suddenly the ball went down the cellar so Tyra and I went downstairs and I saw a machine. I reached my hand to the switch and turned it on with Tyra right next to me. Suddenly a bright beam of light hit us in our foreheads and switched our bodies around, so Tyra and I went outside.

All I could see were black and white figures all over the place and Tyra, in my body, went to see my parents. My mam said in delight, 'Are you enjoying the party?'

All Tyra said was, 'Woof, woof.'

This went on until my mam said, 'You're grounded.'

I ran full charge at my body, through the table and switched our bodies back.

I, in my own body, ran and told my mam the story from start to finish and she did not believe it until my uncle explained it thoroughly to my mam and dad.

Aaron Moon (12)
Eston Park School, Middlesbrough

The Big Cup Final

FA Cup Final. Manchester 4, Arsenal 2. Match report by Wayne Smith.

It was the 'big match' but Man U dominated the whole match. Rooney played a through ball and van Nistelrooy scored past Lehmann after two minutes. Then Wes Brown gave away a penalty to Arsenal and got sent off but Henry missed but scored the rebound. Then came a free kick to Man U on the edge of the box and Cristiano Ronaldo scored to make it 2-1 to United.

Then Rooney made it 3-1 to Man U.

Then on 74 minutes Rooney finished it, off 4-1 to Man U.

Henry scored with 10 minutes to go.

Sadly for Arsenal Henry got injured and Lehmann was sent off for fighting.

Reyes, on for the injured Henry, five minutes later got sent off for fighting. This made it worse for Arsenal.

The full-time whistle went. Malcolm Glazer's and Wayne Rooney's first cup with Man U!

When the Man U players lifted the cup, the Arsenal players left the pitch crying.

Wayne Smith (12)
Eston Park School, Middlesbrough

The Goddess Of Life

We have reason to believe that there is another goddess that we didn't know about until now.

Laurium, the goddess of life, was supposed to have lived around the time of Venus, goddess of love. But Laurium was never seen or heard because of her powers; she would have been chased by people to help them. Laurium was a beautiful, clever goddess but could not reveal this beauty. So she hid in a place in Mount Olympus, only coming out to help people.

Laurium had the power to give life to dead people who hadn't deserved to die. But when she revived them they were in an animal form. This caused a problem because there were becoming more animals than humans.

The gods decided that something had to be done so they told her that she had to stop using her powers or they would make her. But the problem was that Laurium knew that she was doing good so she refused to stop.

The gods were furious so they locked her in her palace so she couldn't use her powers. The gods were then happy but Laurium was not happy and tried to break free but no matter what she did she could not get out.

Laurium is still locked away to this day. Every time you hear thunder and lightning, the thunder is Laurium banging on the gates to get out and the gods throwing lightning at the gates to keep her in.

Laura Hughes (12)
Eston Park School, Middlesbrough

Short Story

Once upon a time there was a king who had just moved into a new castle and he had lived there for just over a week.

There was a room that he had not been in yet and he decided to have a look. He opened the door of the room. All he could see was a very, very big time machine.

In the room there was a huge window and there were parts of machinery all over the floor and everywhere else.

The time machine was a car; it looked like a racing car. The king stepped into the time machine. Inside were lots of buttons and switches. The king pushed a button. Suddenly he was in Spain . . .

Spain was like a dream world. There were trees and flowers everywhere. The sun shone all the time and the houses were beautiful. There were swimming pools and beautiful sights and views. They were amazing.

Spain is beautiful from top to bottom!

Daniel Redmond (11)
Eston Park School, Middlesbrough

A Day In The Life Of Ronaldo

Ronaldo's day started when he woke up at 7am because he had a big match to train for. As soon as he got out of bed he went downstairs to get a healthy breakfast before he went to get ready.

Ronaldo arrived at the ground at 10am to train before his cup game kicked off. When he got in he went to see Alex to find out what the team was for the day. He saw that he was playing so he went to see his teammates. After a while they went outside to train before the supporters came in. After they had trained for two hours they went in to see the manager.

Alex told them all to get stuck into their opponents because of the last game when 'Boro won 2-1. They all told Alex they would. Then the team stayed in the changing room until it was time to go out for kick-off at 1pm.

When kick-off time came they went out onto the field and there was a massive roar from the crowd, because it was a cup final. It was very tense when the whistle blew for kick-off.

It was a close game but Manchester United won 4-2 and Ronaldo scored the winner.

After the match they went into the changing room and Alex told them how well they had done.

Bradley King (11)
Eston Park School, Middlesbrough

Alien Chucky

'Whoops, I've pressed the wrong button,' I said, watching the engine. I'm always clumsy on the spaceship Orion. It's an unlucky ship.

'Chucky, you're dumb and stupid. Why did you do that?'

I knew that Chacky wanted me to answer but I didn't. I'm cleverer than him.

'We're going to crash-land on Earth. It's your fault.'

I'd decided to crash-land on Earth. Something big, I read the people of Earth's minds. They were watching the 2012 London Olympics. Chacky said if I didn't cause destruction, I wasn't going home! Shocking! I went straight to this place. Killed everyone on my way with my laser eyes, moved towards the racetrack, then I made my entrance.

Everyone stopped to stare. I read some more minds. One of them was thinking, *an orange slime ball with three evil eyes can't scare me!* I sure scared him. I killed him with my laser eyes.

Everyone ran towards the exits but the race had to go on. So they started the race. I soon showed them, except one person called Paula Radcliffe; she zoomed past me and kept going; I tried to kill her but she was too fast. I went up to her later to say, 'Wow, you're a quick runner. You were so fast I couldn't kill you.'

'Well, don't kill me,' she begged.

I'm on my way back to my planet Psyche. I never knew that I'd make a new friend. It's Paula. It won't be the last time she'll see me!

Olivia Thompson (12)
Eston Park School, Middlesbrough

'My Story' By The Lady of Shalott

Life had never been easy. When I was a young girl I would sit looking at my mirror, watching the children playing, knowing I would never have that. I would never have friends. I had been cursed since I was a baby. My parents would never tell me why I was cursed. It was always a bit of a dull subject.

Anyway, it was a bright, sunny day and I sat and worked on my tapestry while looking in the mirror. When I saw Lancelot riding past, I fell madly in love and, for the first time in my life, I forgot the curse and turned to the window! My tapestry exploded and I knew the curse had begun to take place.

I ran down to the river and sat in a little wooden boat. I carved my name on the side of the boat so Lancelet would know who I was. When night fell, I untied the boat and drifted upstream. By the time I was halfway up the river, I was dead!

Now I wander between two worlds looking, waiting for Lancelot and I will not pass to Heaven until I am complete. Until I have Lancelot.

Nicola Coates (12)
Eston Park School, Middlesbrough

Achilles' Heel

The Greek king, Menelaus, was preparing for battle with the Trojans. Paris, the Prince of Troy had just been to visit him, but while Paris was visiting, he had an affair with King Menelaus' wife, Queen Helen. She left Menelaus and went with Paris.

Messengers were dispatched across the land to the best fighters. One was sent to Achilles with a request from King Menelaus, 'Will you fight for me in the Trojan War? Do you accept the challenge?' Achilles was a brave and honourable soldier so he accepted.

The Trojans lost many of their men to him and were afraid to fight. After a couple of years fighting in the war, Achilles had an argument with King Agamemnon over a captive maiden so he withdrew his army and sulked in his tent.

The Trojans took advantage of his absence and attacked the Greeks, driving them headlong into retreat. Then Patroclus, Achilles' best friend, begged Achilles to let him wear his armour. The Trojans retreated in fear when they saw Patroclus in Achilles' armour.

As the Trojans retreated, Patroclus tried to take Troy but was killed in combat by Prince Hector.

Achilles was distraught at the news and returned to the battle. He died after being shot in the ankle, which was the only place that he was not immortal after being dipped in the River Styx by his ankles as a child.

Kate Stephenson (12)
Eston Park School, Middlesbrough

The Lady Of Shalott

Once upon a time,
In the town of Camelot,
Lived a woman called,
The Lady of Shalott

She had long, straight hair,
She had a beautiful face,
She had a snow-white dress,
She moved with grace

She had beads round her neck,
A band around her head,
Some patterns on her gown,
But had no street cred.

She had nice white shoes,
And was rather tall,
With a gold ring,
And a white shawl.

But the Lady of Shalott,
She was under a curse,
But she wasn't just locked in a tower,
This was worse

Because she could not directly see,
The town of Camelot,
She had to look through a mirror
Did the Lady of Shalott.

David Siddaway (13)
Eston Park School, Middlesbrough

The Lady Of Shalott

The Sun has been told that the Lady of Shalott was found dead on a boat about 5 o'clock this morning.

Some friends reported that she'd died because of the curse but others asserted that she was poisoned.

We have also been told that the reason she left her room was because she saw the brave knight, Sir Lancelot, riding past her window, through her mirror, and she wanted to see him properly, although this has not been confirmed.

She allegedly ran to her boat and began to float towards Camelot. As she floated past Camelot all the knights saw her and made crosses but Sir Lancelot reportedly said, 'She has a lovely face'.

Her friends said the reason that she was killed by the curse was because she had told them that when she was a baby a witch put a curse on her so that she could only see the world through a mirror and if she looked away from the mirror she would die!

Callam Stevenson (13)
Eston Park School, Middlesbrough

The Shadow Poet

Do you know the curse of the Lady of Shalott? Well, long, long ago and far, far away is where my story starts.

There was once a lady trapped in a tower. The room she was locked in was dark, gloomy and damp with only one window. Unfortunately this lady was cursed and never allowed to look out of the window. But the Lady of Shalott was very clever. She had placed her mirror on an angle so she could see outside the window through the mirror.

One very beautiful afternoon, when the sun was shining bright and the flowers were bursting with colour, a shadowy figure appeared in the reflection. It was rather odd for the lady because she never had visitors. The figure began to speak to himself. He almost recited it. He said,

'You are my summer's
day
More temperate and
lovely
Like the darling buds
of May.'

At once the Lady of Shalott knew she was in love. For the next fourteen days the figure would come and say the lovely verses of poetry. It was as if he knew her or even as if he loved her. But she knew the poems were not meant for her but that didn't stop her listening.

'But summer doesn't
last all year long
You're more like a human
heaven
And this is why I write
this song.'

The Lady of Shalott had never felt this way before. How could she be in love with a dark shadow? She knew she had to turn to look. So on the fourteenth day he came and he said,

'I love you,
Please love me
Sometimes the very thing
you're looking for
Is the one thing you can't
see.'

And with that the lady turned around to see the man she had fallen in love with. Now she had seen him she knew she would have to find her resting place. Then she remembered one of the Shadow's poems. It had mentioned 'The first time I saw you, floating down the lake, I knew I was in love'.

She ran down to the nearest lake and got into a little boat. She lay herself down and eventually fell asleep, never to awaken.

Natalie Cronin (13)
Eston Park School, Middlesbrough

The Lady Of Shalott

There once was Lady of Shalott
Her face was pale and milky
Her hair, long, uncut and ginger
Her skin was soft and silky

She was very young and pretty
But she had an evil witch's curse
It was put on by a nasty witch
The witch put it on and showed no remorse

The curse said she could not see the world
Only through the looking glass
Then one day a prince went walking by
He let his horse graze on the grass

He was called the Prince of Camelot
She really quite liked the prince
So she decided to look out of the window
And she broke the curse without a wince

She jumped out of the window
But the prince was well gone
She stood and peered around
Now she was dying and alone

She did not know what to do
So she took a big, fancy boat
Still looking for her charming prince
She sat on the wooden seat and set afloat

Down the long blue river she went,
The curse started to take effect
Eventually it got too bad and she died
Her boat, soon in a current, was wrecked

The prince then found her young body
He thought that this tragedy was a disgrace
He thought that she was a charming gal
And that she had 'a lovely face'.

Tania Culley (13)
Eston Park School, Middlesbrough

The Lady Of Shalott

From down the tower she looked upon,
the kingdom which was far beyond.
A place of joy and merry song,
where happiness and joy belong.
The kingdom of Camelot.

She spat upon their merry land,
with fire in heart and mirror in hand.
She hated them and their castles, grand
The Lady of Shalott.

The people were but quite upset,
for the cursing and taunting without regrets.
So they plotted against the wretch,
so the world she knew, she would forget.
The people of Camelot.

Through a mirror she would see,
for out the window death would be.
Cursed and destroyed was she
The Lady of Shalott.

Benjamin Rutledge (13)
Eston Park School, Middlesbrough

A Day In The Life Of The Lady Of Shalott

For once in my life I'd love to see,
Beyond this room that belongs to me.
Instead of looking through a looking glass,
I'd love to see, smell and touch the grass.
I'm sick of living in this small room,
It's always full of sadness and gloom.

Sir Lancelot who I love so much,
I'm sick of my sight I'd love to touch.
I am limited to just my sight,
Every time he comes past I take flight.
Temptation has got the best of me,
I looked away cos I had to see.

Can this be real and can it be true?
Out of that room now the sky is blue.
Even though my time is over,
I might find my four-leafed clover.
To help me leave the curse behind,
To help me have a peaceful mind …

I then floated down to Camelot,
Where I did see my Sir Lancelot.
I lay pale and still, I will be forgot.

Launa McGlade (13)
Eston Park School, Middlesbrough

The Picnic

My mum and dad had sent me to stay at my grandparents' house whilst they redecorated our house. Even though I loved my grandparents I had been there for ten days and was beginning to get extremely bored. Grandad suggested we take a picnic and explore the mysterious woods which lay beyond their house. I asked my grandad if it was scary in the mysterious woods. My grandad said he didn't know but there had been different strange stories about the gloomy woods.

We set off the next day. As we were walking I started to panic a little bit because of what my grandad had told me, even though I thought it might be fun in the woods.

I saw lots of mysterious things like snakes and jumping spiders talking. Grandad and I sat down and had our picnic, we had our best sandwiches and cakes.

Suddenly, the ground opened and a strange creature came out from the dark depths of the earth. It had a huge eye on the top of its scaly head. Its teeth were like razor blades and its body was green and slimy. My grandad and I were scared.

The creature grabbed our picnic then disappeared back into the ground. We had seen the picnic monster!

We went back to tell Grandma such a tale and to get some more food!

Melissa Hugill (12)
Eston Park School, Middlesbrough

The Lady Dies

The Lady of Shalott died yesterday. She'd come out of her tower. Sir Lancelot was the first person to pass her body. Her tower block is just down the river from King Arthur's palace. We've heard that all she did all day was weave and sew from what she could see outside her window. Unfortunately we cannot reveal her name as nobody knew it.

The king has politely quoted, 'I did not ever see the lady come out of her tower, not once. People have always wondered what she looked liked and was really like herself'. The king has told us, 'People had only seen her as she looked in the mirror and it was reflected back to the window. I don't think she ever directly looked out of the window'.

Some people believe she was cursed but what did this curse mean? Could it mean she couldn't look at other people? Could it mean she couldn't leave her house or look out of the window? Nobody knew apart from the lady herself.

Sir Lancelot claimed she was rowing down the river when she just stopped. On the boat she'd engraved, 'The Lady of Shalott'!

Callie Jo Lowes (11)
Eston Park School, Middlesbrough

Dazzling Death!

The body of the Lady of Shalott was found floating down to Camelot today.

Not much is known about this graceful person apart from her living in a castle situated on the island of Shalott (near the river leading to Camelot) hiding away.

She sang beautiful songs in her soft, sweet voice every day, watching the world go by in her silver mirror.

It has not yet been confirmed whether this was a murder or the suicide of this dazzling woman, but it appears that she had drowned. A boat was found floating nearby, engraved with the words, 'The Lady of Shalott'.

Lancelot, one of King Arthur's best (and best-looking) knights, appeared at the scene and sighed. 'She has a lovely face, God in His mercy lend her grace, the Lady of Shalott'.

Laura Henderson (11)
Eston Park School, Middlesbrough

A Day In The Life Of Crunchie The Dog

Today was fine, then I got up!

Oh, I'll just have 40 winks. It can't harm anybody. Look who's coming into the kitchen! My human pet, Kate! What's that on the table she's picking up? It's the *lead!* How come she's not saying, 'Walkies'? She looks a bit on the worried side. On no! Run for your life, run for your life. It's … it's the vets! I run as fast as I can. Ha, ha, missed me by a mile! I run, I dodge, I jump, I … get caught! *Nooo!* On goes the lead that takes me to Hell. Goodbye mud-stained chair, goodbye garden, goodbye house. Hello stupid car.

Round and round go the wheels, on and on the road stretches. Then (the part I've been dreading) stop goes the car. I feel Kate lift me up and she locks the car.

'Now Crunchie,' says Kate, 'I'd like you to be good.'

I wonder why? It's not as if I'm meeting 'Lassie the wonder dog'! I wish!

We go into reception and Kate says something to a woman in a silly white coat. She smiles and ushers us into a room. Look at all these dogs, oh, and *cats!* Yuck! I'm glad I'm not a cat! Scratching, flea-bitten things that unfortunately landed here because no other planet wanted them! Disgusting creatures! Yuck!

Then Kate smiles and says to me, 'It's OK Crunchie, you're only getting wormed.'

Oh, phew, what a relief!

Amy-Louise Foulkes (12)
Eston Park School, Middlesbrough

The Figure

It was a cold, dark night and it was thundering and lightning. The wind was howling and it was very black and dull. I locked the doors and made a cup of tea and some toast and started to watch the television.

I went to close the curtains and I saw a strange figure looking directly at our house. I told my mam. She checked the locks on all the doors and windows. I went up the stairs and looked out of my bedroom window to see if the figure was still there and to my surprise it was. I looked down the street and then I saw the figure walking away.

We never saw that person or figure again. Shortly afterwards we moved house.

Jodi Turner (11)
Eston Park School, Middlesbrough

The Lucky Cat

One sunny afternoon Sarah was in the back garden picking apples off her tree. Sarah had loads of different trees. She had two apple trees, two banana trees, two pear trees and one orange tree.

All of a sudden she saw a cat run past. When Sarah had picked twenty apples she went inside and locked the door. She saw through the window that the cat was on one of her trees.

The next day Sarah had to go and pick some pears. Every time she picked one off the tree, another one appeared. After Sarah had picked twenty pears she went inside and rinsed them.

Every day for the next four days the same thing kept happening. On the fifth day Sarah went out and put the lottery on while the cat was on the tree. When she got back, the cat was still on the tree.

Later that night when the lottery was being drawn, Sarah realised that the cat was again on the tree. Every number that came up Sarah had! Now all she needed was the bonus!

'Yes!' She had it.

From that day forward Sarah called the cat, 'The Lucky Cat'!

Megan Dales (12)
Eston Park School, Middlesbrough

Ned Kelly Or Mark Schwarzer?

Middlesbrough go into the European Cup for the second time in a row. Jimmy Floyd Hasselbaink put 'Boro ahead in the 23rd minute with a wonderful free kick.

Manchester City wearing their new away kit, troubled 'Boro's defence but 'Boro must have gone to sleep at half-time and did not even wake up when Musampa just walked through and scored the equaliser in the 47th minute.

David James played up front for the last ten minutes. Every time he kicked the ball at least three 'Boro players were on the floor.

Man City were awarded a penalty kick in stoppage time and Robbie Fowler's shot was fantastically saved by Schwarzer.

'Boro pulled through and made it to Europe and let's hope we're in Cardiff next season.

Austin Sisson (12)
Eston Park School, Middlesbrough

A Day In The Life Of Me

'Come on Kate, it's time to get up!' my mum calls, popping her head round the door.

I groan and bury my head in the pillow.

'Kate, come on, you've got to get ready for ...'

'OK, I'm getting up!' I interrupt her and sit up in bed. This convinces her that I'm getting up and she leaves the room. As soon as I hear the door shut, I drop back down and try to resume the pleasant dreams I'd had a few minutes ago.

School mornings always start that way. When I eventually get up, I clamber about like a zombie and subconsciously dress myself.

I'm on my way to first lesson now, history. The corridor is buzzing with noise, and as usual, people are pushing and shoving their way past. Ouch! I've just felt a Rockport squash my foot. Finally! I've reached the classroom and I sit down. The lesson passes quickly and before I know it, I'm on my way to maths. This lesson always seems to pass agonisingly slowly, so I'm relieved when I hear the bell go for break.

I don't remember much about the rest of the lessons, except for making shortcake in food technology, which is now in a box on my knee as I'm on the bus home. I'm so happy now because it's Friday, which means I don't have to go to school tomorrow, or the day after. (I will not let myself think about Monday yet!)

Kate Pearson (12)
Lord Lawson of Beamish School, Birtley

A Long Way Home

A tear slipped down my cheek. I gulped, but they kept coming. He waved at me as the train left the station. I felt empty, like someone had stolen something. The travellers vanished. The only person I could see was Luke. I forced a smile and bit my lip; so did he. He mouthed something to me when the train bumped round the corner. I was puzzled. I became frustrated and tried to remember his words. I was never good at lip-reading.

The train had gone now and was completely out of sight. I swallowed and stared at where he'd been standing. I heard a beep, then remembered the taxi waiting. I went to the taxi stand and told the driver my address. He nodded and drove off.

In his mirror I could see my face. It was wet and tears began sliding down my cheeks again. The driver turned his radio down, then asked me what the matter was. I swallowed and told him. He gave me a comforting look.

As he drove down my street I relaxed. I told him where to stop and gathered my money. He roared the engine and turned the radio up. I heard a faint click, then realised doors had been locked. He drove past my house. I was horrified, I told him to stop. He still ignored me when I banged on the windows, and stared at the passers-by, but I only got blank looks in return. The music was still playing …

Lena Platow (12)
Lord Lawson of Beamish School, Birtley

A Day In The Life Of A Fish

Today I started my journey of life. This would be the day I would follow my ancestors, grandparents and my mother and father. This is me that, well that is the hardest thing in a fish's life. We all gathered, I had seen nothing like it before; there were tens of thousands of us there to witness the biggest adventure ever.

One minute to go: the stream was perfect. *Go! Go! Go!* We were off, it felt like I was flying, flying off the top of the world. My heart was pounding like a wild cheetah going after its prey.

Suddenly I bumped into someone. 'Bling, is that really you?'

'Karl! I haven't seen you for two years.'

Bling was my best mate when we were young, I have known him since I was a baby; he was born right next to me. 'How are you doing these days?' I asked.

'Like always, fit as a fiddle.'

'OK then, are you ready to get back to our journey?'

'Yeah, we should really get back because we don't want to be late.'

'Come on then, let's go.'

After a few minutes we were back on track. We whizzed past all of the other fish like they were cars on a motorway.

'Look Bling, there it is on the horizon, I can see it, it's Heaven.'

We raced to get there. We smashed against the current in the river, but eventually we made it to our new home, the ocean.

Karl Richardson (12)
Lord Lawson of Beamish School, Birtley

Dreaming

One dark night in the little house on Louden Street, the lightning furiously struck, the rain fell from the gloomy sky like bombs. The hand-like trees tapped at the window of Lucy's room as she lay in bed, dreaming about her dad. It was a long, sad year ago when her dad went missing. Friday the 13th 2004. He was later found ... dead! No one knows how this happened, or who did it. She felt like she had drowned in her tears over the year and only wanted her dad. Finally she got to sleep.

She got woken a few hours later by the chimes of the clock striking midnight. She tried to get back to sleep, but mysteriously heard the voice of her dad. She thought she was dreaming, but no.

'I'm in the bathroom, Lucy.'

She was so afraid.

He spoke again, *'Lucy, I'm on the landing, I want to see you again. I've missed you so much.'*

'Leave me alone, go away,' Lucy screamed.

'Lucy, I'm coming to see you.'

Suddenly, a spooky cold breeze came into her room and made her shiver like a freezing Eskimo. There he was, standing in the doorway.

'There you are. I love you so much.'

Lucy ran as fast as she could to her dad, but he vanished ... Lucy woke up. Her dad had gone forever, it was all a dream. She felt like her heart had been taken away from her. She went back to bed and wept ...

Lauren Riley (12)
Lord Lawson of Beamish School, Birtley

A Day In The Life Of Baz, The Alsatian Dog

6.30am - My master wakes me up and gives me a cuddle and a hello, then he takes me to get clean before the long journey. He takes me to the car, where I jump into the boot. (That's where I stay for a while!)

7.30am - We arrive at Ponteland, where I get clean again then we get to work training, like catching the ball and searching, things like that. (My favourite is biting people with weapons and protective gear!)

12 noon - Dinner time, well at least for my master. I just get a break to chat with my mates to hear the latest gossip!

3pm - Time to go home. My master says goodbye to his pals and I say bye to mine, then I jump into the boot to go homeward-bound.

5pm till 10pm - Well, this is my free time. It's a bit boring though, Katherine comes to play with me, I get my dinner and I go for a walk. I think it's supposed to tire me out and it works. I drift softly to dreamland.

Katherine Saunders (11)
Lord Lawson of Beamish School, Birtley

Anny And The Minotaur

It was horrible. It was chasing me. It had the head of a bull and legs that looked just like mine. Human legs! Running and running as fast as I could, swerving and winding round the rough maze trying to find a way out. 'Wrong way!' I said as I scurried out to find another route. *Oops!* I thought. *It knows where I am now.* It was there, in front of me, all scruffy and ragged! I was dead. Deader than dead. Not yet, I needed to run, run away, but I couldn't. It was growling and scuffing its hooves on the dusty ground. It ran at me. Yes, I jumped on top of a hedge. Ooh! Yes. 'Ha, ha, you can't get me now.'

I was over two metres high above the thing, so there was no chance of it getting me. It growled and howled and then went away. I was so petrified. It was all over!

I jumped down from the hedge as quietly as I could and I crept and hid behind every hedge, trying to find an opening. I jumped on top of the tallest hedge and I could see an opening. I was free to go back home. My parents hadn't seen me in two days.

Right, turned left, then I went straight forward, then turned right and left again. Ooh, then I was at the clearing.

I got down as quietly as a mouse and went to the clearing. It was waiting there!

Denise Scott (11)
Lord Lawson of Beamish School, Birtley

'The Lord Of The Rings' VS 'Harry Potter'

'Fire!' shouted Legolas as some unwanted visitors entered the forest of Mirkwood. There was a war between the wizards of Earth and the beings of Middle-Earth. The leaders of Middle-Earth are Legolas, Prince of Mirkwood, Aragorn, King of Gondor, Gimli, cousin of Balin and Gothmog, cunning captain of the Orcs.

Harry Potter led the wizards. 'We think that the elves are cloaked!' exclaimed Harry.

A large white owl called Hedwig flew overhead. Harry gave her a message and she glided away. The elves spotted her and attempted to shoot her down. They failed.

'Grrrrr,' grumbled Gimli, 'I think I know where she is heading.'

The owl was heading to the iron hills, a place that the wizards had already claimed from the dwarves in a previous battle. She called extra wizards to Mirkwood. The wizards were too worried about the battle at Mirkwood to realise that their settlement would be undefended and open to attacks from Gothmog's army from the south.

Word got to the wizards that reinforcements were on their way. The wizards in Mirkwood charmed their wands to warn them of any hidden elves along the way. The reinforcements were late.

'We need more wizards to claim Mirkwood,' said Harry.

Near the Running River, the wizards got ambushed by rangers hiding in the wood.

Harry went to battle.

'Reclaim the iron hills, you maggots!' ordered Gothmog.

Legolas fired three arrows and killed Harry. The wizards were lost, so they retreated. Peace was restored to Middle-Earth.

Liam Scott (11)
Lord Lawson of Beamish School, Birtley

Prince Charles And The Knights Of The Triangular Table

Prince Charles was extremely unhappy. His only love, Camilla, didn't love him! Instead, she had set him one task, it being to find a triangular table. Where in the world would he find one? Prince Charles was very rich though (he was, after all, a prince). He was so rich that he had a magical portal into another dimension, called Narnia. Although Charles had never ventured into Narnia, he knew there was a triangular table, but he also knew there was a wicked witch so powerful she could turn anything, or anyone, into jelly. You can imagine, he was very scared but he had to complete the task, so in he went through the portal and onto the crisp snow.

He walked down the yellow-bricked road and eventually he got to a clearing. There, standing on the triangular table, was the red witch! Around her stood six knights, all turned to jelly. Charles leapt behind the witch and took her wand. Instantly the witch turned to jelly and all the knights around her turned back to normal.

'Knights of the Triangular Table, let's go!'

Once back home, Charles asked Camilla to marry him. The Queen wasn't too happy, but she offered Camilla a trip to Paris, all expenses paid!

Roseanna Smith (12)
Lord Lawson of Beamish School, Birtley

'Harry Potter' Meets 'Star Wars'

One dark, damp night, a young boy named Harry Potter woke as the clock struck twelve. His scar was burning like the scorching depths of Hell. He crept down the stairs of the house to grab a snack. It was not the Dursley's house, he hated them so much he ran away. He stepped up to the fridge when a figure emerged from the darkness. It was Sirius Black! Harry shouted, 'You betrayed my parents and they were your friends!'

Sirius spoke, 'Harry I am your godfather.'

Harry screamed, *'Nooooo!'*

Harry ran into the dark forest to find Obi Wan about to slay Hedwig. Harry yelled, 'Stop!' and blasted Obi Wan with lightning. Harry continued to blast, while Obi Wan dodged every shot. Obi Wan leapt into the shadows of darkness. Obi Wan was nowhere to be seen. By then, Hedwig had had the common sense to fly away. Obi Wan jolted out of the shadows and fiercely ran towards Harry.

Out of the distance, Sirius emerged. Sirius blasted lightning straight at Obi Wan, but it deflected off Obi Wan's light sabre and zapped Harry with 1,000,000 volts! Harry fell to the ground with a burnt face and stuck-up hair.

Harry spoke, 'The day I die, and I don't even get to have breakfast!'

A funeral was arranged; Harry's body was cremated. Harry's friends and companions were there, except for Ron, whose flying car had run out of petrol on the motorway.

Sam Thoburn (12)
Lord Lawson of Beamish School, Birtley

A Day In The Life Of Arthur Gold

Arthur got up out of his silky golden bed and strolled downstairs on his golden staircase, into his kitchen to have a cup of Nescafé Gold Blend. As he sipped his coffee, Arthur thought to himself, *if it wasn't gold, it wasn't good.*

Arthur was a lonely man because there were no other Goldiacs on the planet. And just like his coffee, if people weren't gold they weren't good enough for him either.

He sat down to do his golden oldie crossword with his sparkly golden pencil. Gold was his only friend in this world. 'One across, hmmm. Three letters, primary colour, starts with 'R'. *Who invented these damned impossible crosswords?'* he bellowed to the heavens. So Arthur decided to go out to relieve his stress level to buy a few packets of McVities Gold biscuits and five tubs of St Ivel Gold spread.

People started to stare and wonder if he was wrong in the head, with his golden face paint, golden joggers and his sparkly golden jumper.

He started to murmur under his breath, 'Lower class, out-of-fashion toe-rags.'

As Arthur walked home, on his own as usual, there was a sudden downpour of rain. The raindrops were huge, bouncing high off the pavement. Cars going past showered Arthur with dirty rainwater, he was furious once again! Arthur looked down to find he was going rusty. 'Hey, I thought gold didn't rust ...'

Alex Turnbull (12)
Lord Lawson of Beamish School, Birtley

Ghost

It all started when Don Smith was murdered outside his house. His wife had come back from a party and seen him hanging from his balcony down to the front of the door.

A week later, when the police had stopped coming round asking questions, and the forensic criminalists had stopped taking pictures of the crime scene, weird things started to happen ...

One night the widow, Melissa, was sobbing while watching TV, then suddenly she heard, *bang!* She shot up and slowly walked into the kitchen, but there was nothing there, so she made herself a cup of tea and sat back down. She put the cup on the table beside her, but when she went for another drink, it was on the floor.

Half an hour later she went up to bed. Melissa was trying to get to sleep, but she could hear banging and footsteps in the attic, so she called her best friend, Danni. Danni was trying to calm her down, but then the line cut off and it began to thunder and lightning. She kept saying to herself it was all just a bad dream.

The next morning Melissa woke from having a nightmare about how her husband died. While she was in the shower, she heard the phone ring. Melissa got out of the shower, but it was too late. The door banged open and all the neighbours could hear was a scream ...

Sarah Young (12)
Lord Lawson of Beamish School, Birtley

Crook'd Hall

I didn't believe in ghosts until I visited the haunted Crook'd Hall. You're probably thinking, *haunted, hmmm … like that's true,* but that's what I thought until …

'We're here, get out of the car,' said my mam.

I got out and looked around the gardens. At 2.30, there was to be a ghost hunt, which I thought was rubbish. The ghost was supposed to be 'The White Lady'. There was a person that kept popping up, but she had a Livestrong band on, which gave it away big time. So it was either someone dressed up, or ghosts support cancer research. I told my mam it was boring and said I'd meet her later. I took a wrong turn, to find myself lost. I tried to ring my mam, but my battery had run out. 'Argh!' I shouted in rage. I slumped against the wall feeling sorry for myself.

A strong voice from behind me said, 'Be ye lost, young 'un?'

'Yes,' I replied.

'Aye, I be lost too, follow thee.'

I followed him around a corner, he disappeared and I was back with the group. I was just in time for the last story. Apparently, a medieval soldier was murdered in the room, and the body had been hidden behind a wall. He was said to be a bad man, but I knew different. He was just like me and looking for a way out.

I could never admit to my mam that I believed in ghosts, could I?

Joe Walker (12)
Lord Lawson of Beamish School, Birtley

Untitled

The bright, blinding moonlight gleamed over Alex as he slowly got off the school bus. Alex was late, so he decided to take a short cut through a mysterious forest. As Alex cautiously entered the black, cold forest, an icy, shivery chill shot down his bony spine. Alex had second thoughts, but he knew he had to get home. He slowly wandered through the forest until a black and sorrow-filled shadow shot over the forest like a tidal wave. It was so dark, it was like an eclipse. Alex was petrified and started to spring through the forest like a cheetah. As Alex ran through, he heard horrible moaning sounds and the dark, crooked trees glared at him with their evil eyes. Their old, deformed branches scratched against him like witches' nails.

Alex then encountered a misty cave. He slowly and cautiously crept towards it as the ice-cold wind blew on his pale, frightened face. When he entered the cave, it crumbled like biscuits and suddenly a horrific feeling struck through him and seemed to poison his heart with black madness and sorrow. Alex felt horrific. He miserably staggered up a hill as the cold mist wrapped around his straining ankles.

Alex stared into the vast distance seeing a wet, crooked path. He smiled faintly, seeing an exit, until he tumbled to the mossy, crumbling ground and his pain finally stopped.

Jack Wilkinson (11)
Lord Lawson of Beamish School, Birtley

Red Shot

This is my moment, he thought. *Our moment; the suffering of our country and our people will end in the next few minutes. Finally freed from self-righteous tirades, self-serving policies and globalisation.*

The assassin readjusted the viewfinder of his sniper rifle. It would not be long now. He thought of previous new years; the parties, the drink, the women. Never did he expect that new year 2007 would be sat atop the Santa Moriana Hotel, armed, and prepared to assassinate for the cause of his 'Red Brothers'. It was superbly planned; intricate and timed to perfection.

The assassin's wife and children would be at home, sitting in the front room, Christmas decorations and presents still scattered across the floor in the vibe of the holiday season. They were unaware of the job he was about to perform, but they would know of it soon enough. As they sat around the television waiting for the new year's speech …

The assassin looked down at his electronic wristwatch, growing anxious and impatient. *Three minutes,* he thought to himself. Three minutes more was all that was left of the intolerable persecution of him and his people, and the rest of the world, had to suffer. In three minutes, the whole of Latin America would rejoice. He thought of his idol: *'Che'.* He would be proud.

It was time. Americans flocked around the podium erected in the centre courtyard of the square, eagerly awaiting the speech. The President stepped out jovially, and the assassin pulled the trigger …

Calum Sherwood (14)
Lord Lawson of Beamish School, Birtley

A Day In The Life Of A Forensic Scientist

'Till death us do part! Say it!' Craig shouted at Justin.

'A pact, in which some will live, others will die,' Justin continued.

'On three. One ... two ... three!' Craig shouted.

Bang! (A gunshot is fired.)

'A body has been found in a ditch near the state of Texas!' a TV crew reported at the scene of the crime.

'Snack time, boys!' Lacie, a forensic scientist, shouted.

'What's that?' Duncan, Lacie's new partner in crime asked, as he looked at the white box in Lacie's hands.

'This is a very important tool,' she said, as she opened the box containing five doughnuts, two chocolate and three strawberry with sprinkles. 'You must be my new partner ... um ...' Lacie paused.

'Duncan!' Duncan finished.

'Let's get to work then ... um ...' Lacie paused again.

'Duncan!' Duncan finished, getting agitated.

'You put your foot where mine goes, and nowhere else,' said Lacie as she ducked under the police 'do not cross' line.

They started down this rocky ditch to where the body was at the bottom. Lacy started down the very narrow, rocky path until she came to a patch on the ground. 'What does that smell like to you?' she asked Duncan.

'It smells like vomit,' he replied.

'Just as I thought, bag some up for the lab,' she told him.

As Lacie got closer to the body, she could smell decay. She carried on towards the body, with Duncan close behind. She knelt down beside the body and examined it. She noticed the body had bloodshot eyes, stab wounds and hand marks around the neck. She also noticed that the victim was missing a finger.

Maryam Armit (13)
Lord Lawson of Beamish School, Birtley

A Day In The Life Of A Schoolboy

Here we go again. My mam is coming in the room getting closer and closer, just ready to go and wake me up from my much-needed beauty sleep. 'Lewis, Lewis, wake up.'

Note to self: put lock on door.

'Lewis, Lewis, wake up now.'

'I'm up, I'm up.' Great, it's Tuesday, my worst day. First I've got English, then maths, but to top it all off, I've got German.

'I've made your porridge.'

Porridge! How on earth can I like porridge? Shows how much my mam knows.

On the bus I met Phillip, the most annoying person I know.

'What ya doin'?' (Here we go again!) 'Go on, tell me what ya' doin'?' he said.

'Go away please. Has anyone ever told you that no one likes you, you're so … irritating! Go away.'

Just for that one moment, I just lost it! I wondered what he would say.

'What ya doin'?'

Oh I give up, I thought. Then the bus came to a sudden halt …

From then on, the day went downhill. First I had Mrs Nonivin, then Miss Boggle, and to top it off, I had a detention with Miss Clark. I was just glad to go home.

Liam Paul Bate (13)
Lord Lawson of Beamish School, Birtley

Don't Mess With Mr T, Fool

It was a warm night in July inside a pub in North Yorkshire. Cliff Richards' 'Summer Holiday' was playing on the jukebox and Mr T was dancing on the dance floor.

Suddenly there was a loud crash and a large American truck came through the wall. Driving the truck was a moose. It got out of the truck and grabbed Mr T and put him in the truck. The moose got in the driving seat and put the truck into reverse. It drove away and after ten minutes reached the motorway. As the moose was driving, it was cackling hysterically, and after one and a half hours, they reached Newcastle airport.

The moose got out of the truck and pulled Mr T out by his gold medallion. Mr T shouted, 'Watch my bling, fool,' but the moose just ignored him and carried on walking into the airport. The moose pulled out two airline tickets and walked over to the gate. The moose then said, 'Get on the plane or die,' and pulled out a gun.

Mr T replied, shouting, 'I ain't getting on no plane, fool.' He knocked the gun out of the moose's hand and then he started to punch the moose until it was unconscious. Mr T then ran onto the runway and jumped into the A-Team van, which was parked there, and drove off into the horizon.

Tim Bloomer (12)
Lord Lawson of Beamish School, Birtley

A Day In The Life Of Brambles,
The Bovingdon Family Cat

'Mam, can you please let me in? I did my business ages ago, I'm freezing. Please?'

Clunk! The door swung open.

'It's about time you let me in.'

'Hello Brambie-kins,' my mam said.

'Don't you Brambie me; just feed me so that I can go to bed!'

I'll walk around Mam's feet for a while until she feeds me. Ooops, nearly tripped her up.

'Brambles, wait your turn. Scott's first,' Mam shouted. 'Get out of the way.'

'Yeah, yeah, I'm starving you know, I'm wasting awayyyyy.'

Thirty minutes later, the fridge door opens and someone feeds me. Hallelujah.

'That was delicious, filled a hole the size of the Grand Canyon. Oh, I hear my snoozy bed calling me. I'll lie this way … nope, on my back sounds better … no definitely not, sprawled out like a chicken … purrfect, time for dreamland!'

One hour later, still in dreamland:

Ding-a-ling-ling.

'Oh no, bells tinkling, must mean some stupid idiot wants to play and I really can't be bothered. Oh my, am I dreaming? A mouse just dropped down from Heaven.'

'Look what I've got for you Brambles,' my mam said.

'Oh mother of mouse heaven, give it to me!'

'Here you go … not.'

'OK, suit yourself, don't give it to me then. I don't want it. I'm just going to clean myself anyway.'

All of a sudden I started to choke. *Cough, cough, splutter, splutter, burp!* 'That's a relief, I didn't lose a life.'

Time for a quick snooze before night exercises.

A long time later …

'Come on Brambles, bedtime, it's time to go out,' my mam said wearily.

'Oh OK then, I do need the loo again, so goodnight and I'll see you in the morning.'

'Night Brams.'

Emma Bovingdon (13)
Lord Lawson of Beamish School, Birtley

Operation: Shadow Snake

Vietnam, a place I'd never heard of, now was my home. Every day I wake up and sleep in this little bamboo hut, and there is the constant fear of a night-strike from the VC guerrillas. The food is terrible, the heat unbearable, but I am here for one purpose - to fight for my country.

'Johnson!' Hey Johnson, wake up, godammit!'

I opened my eyes, I could hear gunfire, they were close, I had the feeling of it. AK47s and SVDs were all I could hear; they were Vietnamese guns.

'Get up, we've got a war to fight!'

I grabbed my uniform and gun, then walked out for a quick, silent, unexpecting attack on the VC.

'I'll take the hill on the far right, Johnson and Mills take the stream.'

'OK,' I said.

Mills crept like a mouse round a cat. 'VC ahead,' Mills whispered.

I nodded. It was still dark. All of a sudden, there was a bomb flash. There were lots of silhouettes - VC silhouettes. I fired and took them all out.

'Mills, hey! Let's get out of here!'

Mills wasn't there, just a guerilla with a handgun. *Bang!* My vision went blurred and I fell unconscious. I never woke again.

Vietnam had won, but all the killing wasn't right, and now we have the wall to remind us all.

Connor Brady (12)
Lord Lawson of Beamish School, Birtley

A Day In The Life Of A Tiger

I could feel the hot blazing sun reflecting off my orange, stripy fur coat as I lay there in the long dry grass of the jungle. My eyes remained shut; I could hear the soft purring of my fellow tigers.

As I stood up, most of the pride did so too. It was early morning, and as I am the leader of the pride, it was my job to make sure the route to the river was clear of any danger.

I set off through the jungle, the tall, lush, green trees shaded my back. I kept a close eye out for any creatures that could be of any danger to my pride. As I continued forward, I heard a loud crack! I swung round to be greeted by a close friend of mine, Sabastein. Together we came to the conclusion the coast was clear. We gathered the pride and allowed them to pass through the jungle to the river.

Whilst we were at the river, the cubs played in the water, their mothers gathered with a watchful eye. Me and Sabastein stood guard. Every now and again, we would roar to warn away any approaching creatures.

Suddenly, halfway between a loud, fierce roar, I heard a gunshot. That could only mean one thing ... *humans!* I ran towards the pack to warn them. They all turned and began to run towards safety. Two cubs were still playing in the water. I ran in and picked one up in my mouth, Sabastein went to get the other.

I managed to return to safety and take the cub back to its mother, but as I was running, I had heard another gunshot. I was still waiting for Sabastein's return. Out of the jungle came running one cub, but no Sabastein. I ran as fast as my paws would carry me back to the river, but as I arrived, I saw three humans take the fur from the corpse of Sabastein.

Why did they do this? The real question being, who's next?

Beth Foster (13)
Lord Lawson of Beamish School, Birtley

Escaped!

I was running. The hallway appeared to grow as I neared its exit. Unexpectedly, a policeman burst through the door.

'Freeze!'

I ignored his orders. As I neared him, he cocked his gun. I seized his wrist and twisted his limb, causing his hand to release the firearm. I forced my fist into his throat. He collapsed. I was now in the courtyard, nearing the wall.

The alarms started, doors opened, armaments started firing towards me. I dived for the top of the wall, ignoring the barbed wire. I dropped down. Shells whizzed past my cranium; one skimmed my exposed arm.

Pain raced through me; I was petrified (which was weird for someone who'd just been in prison). I heard police dogs snarling, ravenous for my flesh. More officers and the dogs darted in my direction. I began sprinting as swiftly as my body would tolerate. They were catching up, so I entered an alleyway, knowing there'd be a means of escape. I had precious little time.

The dogs were at the opening of the alleyway.

'Where is it?' I shouted at myself. 'There you are,' I said joyfully, as I detected the fire escape and some crates. As I climbed, a dog grabbed my leg. I slipped. Only my injured arm lingered on the ladder. Once again pain raced through my body. I grabbed one of the crates and smashed it on the dog's head. Meat spilled out and they began eating it.

I was free!

George McKeating (13)
Lord Lawson of Beamish School, Birtley

Mammy ...

There was once an unfortunate woman whose husband had recently passed away, leaving her and her young child alone and penniless. The woman couldn't cope because they were really poor, so she decided to kill her daughter to save money and to put her out of her misery. She chopped the little girl up with a kitchen knife one night while she was asleep, then she dumped the disgusting remains in the rubbish bin.

A few days later, in her bedroom, the woman was sitting at her dressing table combing her hair, when she heard a faint noise coming from downstairs. She listened out carefully to try and figure out what the noise was. The floorboards of the stairs began creaking, then the faint noise was heard again. It was a sweet, soothing child's voice. She said, 'Mammy, I'm on the first step.'

The woman was listening closely to hear her clearly.

'Mammy, I'm on the third step.' She kept calling out. 'I'm on the seventh step.'

The woman couldn't move because she felt like she as in a trance. The voice seemed so beautiful and soft.

'Mammy, I'm on the thirteenth step.'

A sharp, sudden chill and a nerve-wracking silence hung in the air ...

Then suddenly, the door of the bedroom flung open. The woman froze, staring at the reflection in her mirror. Staring back at her was her young daughter, her body slashed and cut, covered in fresh blood leaking all over the floor. She held a blood-covered kitchen knife in her small palm.

The last thing that was said in the house of the Wilson family was, 'Mammy, I'm going to kill you!'

Neslisah Kilickap (13)
Lord Lawson of Beamish School, Birtley

The Corridor

As I walked along the narrow, lonely corridor, I noticed that the painting at the end was surprisingly missing. I dreaded my uncle finding out, because that would give him another reason to start an argument with me! Out of nowhere I heard a misplaced scream. A chill crawled up my spine and the hairs on the back of my neck stood up. This just gave me a sudden urge to hide from something I did not yet fear. I turned to open the door to one of the many spare bedrooms and stood behind it, waiting for something, but I didn't know what. I began to hear footsteps leading to where I was hiding. My heart started beating so fast it started to hurt. It was like I wasn't in control of my body! Eventually the footsteps ended. I didn't know what was worse, hearing them or not. The door handle of the old oak door started to turn. What was I to do?

Out of nowhere, I heard a familiar voice saying, 'What exactly do you think you're doing?'

To my relief, the voice was my uncle's, but the door handle still turned! A curled hand sprung onto the door, my uncle's head peered round with a happy, yet frightening, smile! Blood started to flood out of his mouth and out of his creamy-white eyes. I screamed like I've never screamed before. I knew no one could hear me, except the murderer of my uncle! But he was about to pay for this terrible crime.

I ran out of the room watching my uncle falling to the floor. I had no time to grieve, because I felt myself running and running. I hadn't even got a clue where I was running to! I turned the corner to the kitchen to get a knife, but I had been beaten by the *man!* I ran back to the corridor to find an easy escape, but before I knew it, the footsteps began again, but angrier, as though the man was running!

I ran into a room, it was hard because you couldn't tell what the room behind the oak door was. I had run into the blood-coloured bathroom and turned to see the only escape route was the window. But I was on the third floor! I would just be signing myself to death! I ran back into the royal blue hallway. I ran in a panic to the opposite room, which turned out to be the old maid's bedroom.

I could remember not long ago she got fired because of some unknown reason that my uncle wouldn't say. Anyway, I had been sent to watch her pack her very few belongings, just in case she stole some of our valuables. She had thrown her bedding into the laundry chute. I looked round the room searching for it, but it had probably been blocked up when we got the house redecorated.

The footsteps stopped. I ran to the window. The door handle turned. I opened the window. The door opened. I jumped!

Louise Jones Parker ... died, source of death unknown ... probably tortured ... body not found!

Kelly Hall (13)
Lord Lawson of Beamish School, Birtley

The Ghost Child

Some years ago, a man bought a 'fixer-upper' house, and after several hours' work, decided to eat a cold supper, sleep there, and continue early the next day.

As he was lying in bed, thinking about what to do the next day, he heard the wailing of a small child. Sitting up in his sleeping bag, he looked across the room towards the staircase and saw the figure of a small child, hardly more than an infant, descending the stairs, crying. He called out to it, but it ignored him and passed in front of him and went into the living room.

As he rushed into the room he saw the figure, still crying, pass through the wall next to the fireplace. The wailing sound continued, and then died away. Severely shaken, the man nonetheless went to sleep, but rose early the next morning and attacked the wall where he had seen the phantom leave the room.

Imagine his surprise and horror when he found the skeleton of a young child inside the wall! He promptly called the sheriff's office, who removed the skeleton, and after the necessary paperwork, he and the two officers held a token funeral service at the local graveyard.

That night the man waited expectantly, but saw nothing. However, just as he was beginning to fall asleep, he heard the faint sound of laughter. No visions, just the sound of a child laughing, that was all.

Since then, he has heard nothing else.

Sophie Kennedy (12)
Lord Lawson of Beamish School, Birtley

The Fire And Water Guardians

If you were to look back hundreds of years ago you would be able to find details of a mythical creature. This creature was just like the water guardians, only they lived in hot places with fire. These creatures were only known to live in hot, dry areas unlike the water guardians who were only found at wet and cool places. The two guardians never crossed paths and if they did it was said that it would cause great destruction.

These were amazing creatures and had unmatchable strength. They were extremely large creatures with scaled skin. The fire guardians being a shiny fire-red and the water guardians being a silky sky-blue colour. Their eyes were like beautiful diamonds glistening in the waves of the water and the flames that they hide in. Many people tried to hunt down the creatures but no one seemed to succeed. They set out on a journey that no one knew, but time after time they headed off into the darkness never to return.

The guardians were unbeatable and everyone knew it. So day after day the people tried to come up with a way of stopping the beasts until someone realised that they were not harming them because they enjoyed it, it was because they were only doing their job to protect the place that they lived. And the beasts couldn't last that long could they?

Rebecca Gillan (13)
Lord Lawson of Beamish School, Birtley

A Day In The Life Of Me

Monday, day one of the week. I get up at 6.45am to get ready for hospital. I get up, go downstairs to take my tablets and inhaler before I go and get washed and get my school stuff ready for after treatment. Thirty minutes later I leave to go to the hospital (Royal Victoria Infirmary) with my mum in the car.

I have to go to Newcastle for dialysis, that is when someone has kidney problems and dialysis takes the blood out, cleans it and puts it back. It takes about fifteen minutes to get there and we pass, everybody should know this, St James' Park, Newcastle United's home ground.

We turn up at the hospital and I have to get a needle to be able to have dialysis, it's like a giant sewing needle. The needle will go into my left arm, which isn't an ordinary arm, it's called a fistula, which buzzes. After the needle is in they (the nurses) attach two tubes to the end of the fistula needle, which are different colours. Red means it takes the blood out and blue means it puts the blood back.

This treatment lasts three and a half hours, maybe longer; it depends on your weight. It really drags on. During this time, I will watch TV for about an hour. Then I do school work for a couple of hours. Finally I get dressed for school.

Steven Gardner (14)
Lord Lawson of Beamish School, Birtley

The Battle Of Toshhopkarnies

Long ago in the 1600s there was a dragon called Amadran the Almighty. He guarded the Chinese city of Toshhopkarnies, ruled by the evil emperor Satinous Satris. Amadran was put there after Satris found many were fleeing from his city. He even built 8ft walls around the city and a moat, then a dragon to make sure. If people tried to escape, Amadran ate them for his dinner.

One day a very brave man named Lee Yen Mah and some other brave, strong men decided to try to defeat Amadran. But how? With wit and intelligence. They held secret meetings every week in a cellar underneath a bakery store. Finally they thought of a way to capture Lord Satris and to defeat his dragon, so they set off on the 16th May 1605 and they confronted the emperor.

'Sir ... '

'Why are you not kneeling before me?' asked Satris. 'Am I not important in your lives?' He drew out a sword sharply. 'Answer me!'

Lee stepped forward and bowed. 'Sir, we think that you treat us wrong.'

'Ah citizens' quest to defeat me, again. If you succeed, Amadran my almighty will kill you and my son will take over.'

'We wish to challenge you and your dragon to a duel,' said a member of this secret organisation.

'Yeah and if we win then we'll rule the city!' said another.

'You will never win against us ... ' said the emperor, 'but I feel for you trying. Tomorrow the duel will be ... *go!'*

Jenny Race (12)
Lord Lawson of Beamish School, Birtley

Mysterious Landing!

'Oh my goodness what is that?' I pointed to the sky in amazement. I saw a blinding white light soar through the night sky. It was coming towards me and my friend Carlos. We stood there almost paralysed by the sight. We waited for the huge flying UFO to land. It touched the black soil with an almighty bang making the ground tremble.

Luckily for Carlos and me it landed well away from us in the forest behind the hill. We were curious as to what it actually was so we then ran up the slippery hill to watch.

We both were watching, waiting, hiding behind a small hedge, peeping at the unfamilar goings on.

All of a sudden the large red door opened very wide. Out of the door dropped a silver ladder in which something rather peculiar-looking slid down. By this time we were so transfixed that we just had to watch what else was going to happen.

The obscene creature started coming towards us, its bloodshot eyes bulging, flashing its piercing teeth, then all of a sudden it vanished. Just like that! We felt a huge wave of relief sweep over us, then we realised it must be a trap. It was almost too good to be true, to get away from the beast so easily.

We crept quietly back and saw the alien-type creature at the bottom of the deep, dark pit. Its body, a bony, translucent structure glowed in the dark. The screams and whining of the monster were deafening whelps.

'Argh! What's happening ...'

Kimberley Taylor (13)
Lord Lawson of Beamish School, Birtley

The Black Coach Inn

'This is all your fault Hector,' Florin told his servant, 'not only did you insult him, you also hit him over the head with a pan of boiling oil.'

Hector didn't answer, he knew better than to backchat his master.

'Village up ahead my lord,' called one of the mean arms.

'Hector, go find lodgings,' Florin demanded.

Hector walked off mumbling curses.

'Come here, I have something to tell you,' croaked an old woman. Hector strode closer. 'You shouldn't stay here, it will only bring death.'

'How?' gasped Hector.

'I have already said too much,' replied the old woman as she walked away glancing over her shoulder.

Hector dismissed the incident and headed into the local inn.

'Gather round and hear a tale of knights' honour and death,' bellowed the strange traveller. The traveller continued, 'There once was a brave knight who was a great slayer of evil that tyrannised the world from dragons and wraiths to hydras and witches. He came upon rumours of a traveller who would drain anyone it met dry. The knight leapt at the chance to slay another evil being.

The knight travelled for months looking for the traveller. He finally found the traveller on the outskirts of this village. The knight confronted the monster and it laughed in his face, then smashed the knight to the ground. As the creature leapt for the kill, the knight put his sword through the monster's heart, but in its dying breath the monster bit the knight, spreading its evil seed. To this day the knight takes the place of the traveller.'

'How could you possibly know that?' asked Florin.

'Because,' laughed the traveller, 'I was that knight!' smiling to reveal huge fangs.

There would be no escape. They all knew they were going to die …

Andrew Swaddle (13)
Lord Lawson of Beamish School, Birtley

Pedro's Long Journey

It was Saturday afternoon. I was getting prepared for a long day ahead of me tomorrow. I'd got everything I needed because my essentials that I required were cheaper here.

Anyway, I'm Pedro. I currently live in Mexico but I'm migrating to California as the jobs here are not very well paid and the housing isn't so good either.

It was five o'clock. I had finished my shopping then I was travelling to Acapulco to say my goodbyes to my family because I knew I would probably never see them again, but they all understood my reasons for leaving. I was hoping to be back from Acapulco at about seven so I could have at least eleven hours sleep, as I would really need it for my adventure ahead of me.

'Well this is it,' I said to myself looking at my house for the very last time. It was a really hot, sunny day which I hoped it wasn't going to be because it's always easier to walk in cold weather than hot.

I had been walking for about two hours and I had seen about twenty animals that I'd never come across all the years I'd lived here. I could see for thousands of miles just dusty sand and cactus. It seemed like it would take years to get there but I had made my decision and I was going to stick to it.

About three hours later I came across two men in green overalls and guns by their sides … *the immigration officials.* I didn't think I was that close! I could just see the bank leading down to the Rio Grande, just one of the rivers in Mexico, but I had to swim across to reach my destination. *Bang!* And before I knew it my journey turned very short indeed.

Sophie Stobbart (13)
Lord Lawson of Beamish School, Birtley

A Mystical Encounter

Water dragons beautiful creatures, descendants of the Ben Vair dragons. There has never been a reported sighting of a water dragon … except one day in the year of 1606.

16th May 1606, a handsome knight galloped along the lonely, dusty dirty track astride his bright white horse, his head up with pride. Just as well his mother named him after a famous dragon, Nagas, or he might not have had the confidence to leave home. Nagas had always been interested in dragons. Back in his town of Comunsoon, where his father was dying, Nagas was on his quest to save his father, he didn't know what was in store for him.

As Nagas and his horse, Lightning, entered Soridis forest, Nagas shuddered remembering sinister tales he'd heard about it. On the other side of the forest Monclaw the water dragon was trying to breathe fire but failed. He started whimpering. Nagas had no idea what the noise was and started to panic. Lightning suddenly started running with fear. Nagas fell off her with a loud thud and Lightning, still running, disappeared into the distance.

In the distance Nagas could still hear something unusual; he had nowhere to go so he decided to follow the peculiar sound. In about twenty-five minutes Nagas saw a small clearing, sitting in the clearing was a bizarre-looking small blue creature. It looked like a dragon, but it had scales and very small wings. Just then the creature looked over in Nagas' direction. It had spotted him …

Laura Smith (13)
Lord Lawson of Beamish School, Birtley

The Alien

I woke up in my tent on the fifth day of the expedition. I realised that the temperature had dropped. I stepped out of my tent and walked over to my friend's tent and pulled open the flap. There was nothing there. I lifted up the sheets of the sleeping bag, their was a puddle of blood and some shredded clothes out of the tent.

I woke up the rest of the team and we had no idea what had happened. We searched the area around the tent and all we could find were footprints leading away.

We packed up all our belongings and followed the trail. It led us about one mile south from our camp. We ended up at the entrance of a cave. We stopped and discussed what to do, The cave was dark and there was a chilling breeze leading from the entrance. We wandered into the cave; it was pitch-black. There was something dripping from the ceiling. We turned on our torches and looked up. It was blood.

We then heard a cry from the cave; we ran towards and suddenly it stopped. There was no noise but there was a flickering light a little further ahead. We ran towards it. There was only a small fire burning in the centre of the room. We heard a crunch behind us as we turned around; there was hideous creature standing there. I screamed as it swallowed me whole and then it went black …

Anthony Smith (13)
Lord Lawson of Beamish School, Birtley

A Day In The Life Of My Guinea Pig Houdini

Yawn! The sun's shining through the wire mesh of my hutch. Uh! I bet that sister of mine has pushed me in the corner again and pinched all the hay - typical! I wonder if that lazy girl Rebecca has brought my breakfast yet? Let's go find out. No luck, just a few old bits of carrot from last night. I suppose that'll have to do. Uh oh! There's a noise better dive into the remaining hay in case there is trouble. Wait a minute, what's that smell? Oh! Breakfast has turned up, about time. Better breathe in a bit if I'm to push past my sister and get there first. Ah, nice breakfast, bit full now so I'm just going to close my eyes a bit ...

What's that noise? Oh, Rebecca's home from school already. We must be going on the grass. This could be my chance to escape. Maybe if I wriggle a bit I might just get out of Rebecca's arm. No such luck - she just held on to me tighter. Anyway, this is the life. What more could you want - a jungle of grass, a bit of evening sun, five-star treatment. Uh oh! The sun is going down, looks like bedtime.

So I am hand-carried to my hutch with a bit of cucumber for my supper and I snuggle down in some hay ... the perfect end to a perfect day!

Rebecca Scott (13)
Lord Lawson of Beamish School, Birtley

A Day In The Life Of Mrs Morton

The kids are driving me insane! They don't even bother to listen to me anymore. I got locked in the store cupboard again last night, the laughing was unbearable. They have no respect whatsoever.

I simply can't survive two more weeks of this madness. I got my Bible sent to me as I normally turn to it in times of need but it has not helped me at all this time. Being locked in this classroom with all these children has made me see their true colours.

I didn't sleep a wink last night, they had their music blasting loud right till the early hours. I just simply can't believe the reason why I'm stuck in here, that the class caught a contagious disease and we all have to be locked in this classroom until it's cleared up.

The children are asleep so I am stuck in here until someone wakes up and remembers to get me out.

There is another teacher who has been locked in the classroom as well, Mrs Elsom. She has also tried her best to keep these children under control but neither of us have any effect on them.

Finally, I've been released. It's so bright that the light stings my eyes. The mess is unbelievable, food everywhere, rubbish scattered around. You would never think that these children could have made this mess. They look so peaceful when they sleep, like little angels.

Sarah Winnard (14)
Lord Lawson of Beamish School, Birtley

English Class In Quarantine

It was confirmed 2 days ago that a deadly virus contaminated a school in the north of England.

The attack, thought to be by Al Queda members, was on an English class at Lord Lawson of Beamish School, containing 29 pupils and a teacher.

They are now in quarantine inside the classroom, which has been put in a large tent to stop the virus escaping. The quarantine will last a further 3 weeks while vaccinations are given to everyone in a 15 mile perimeter.

The people inside the classroom are given daily supplies of food and water.

The virus peroxide will slowly eat the body inside to out. A cure is being flown in from America. Each student has been allowed 1 bag containing things from home, all these will be burnt, along with the classroom, on departure.

We managed to get a letter from one of the students inside, which reads:

'On Thursday afternoon we were all tired and ready for home since it was a hot day. Then we heard some shouting and someone run past the door throwing in what we thought was a tennis ball from PE, until it exploded into a cloud of smoke, knocking us all unconscious.

After we all woke up 8-10 hours later, we saw a scientist at the window wearing a biohazard suit. He passed a letter through a small window and it explained what had happened'.

Craig Atherton (14)
Lord Lawson of Beamish School, Birtley

A Day In The Life Of a Soldier In World War II

It was D-Day. Gunfire rained upon us like a hailstorm. I jumped up and started shooting my M141 sub-machine gun. Three Germans fell down, dead. I dropped down into the trenches and ran further through towards the general as a frag landed where I was standing before.

The general ordered to charge. We all ran. Most of my unit died. I had a wounded arm from a German MP44. I fell down so the Germans thought I'd died.

I looked around and saw Lieutenant Colonel Robert Cole who was the commander of the 3rd Battalion, 502nd Parachute Infantry Regiment of 101st Airborne Division. I grabbed his sniper and eyed the German general and shot him in the eye.

The Germans looked around for the killer. I put my head down. I crawled very carefully and quietly back into the trenches. I slipped down and threw a grenade into the German trenches. Luckily I hit some.

I walked to the end of the trenches and set up my new sniper and started to pick them off one by one. Everyone from the German side started to charge. I saw a tank in the distance so I went round the side where no one could see me and I jumped on the tank and put a grenade down the hatch. I ran back and jumped into the German trenches and hid there and shot any German that came.

I made it back to base for the night.

Daniel Tate (12)
Lord Lawson of Beamish School, Birtley

A Day In The Life Of A Victorian Girl

On Tuesday 1st November 1894 I was woken up by my baby brother because he was crying. It was just 5.45am and I felt like sleeping until 10am but I had to get ready for school. I decided to put on my dress, which was scruffy.

My family are very poor. My dad died when I was 4 and my mum is very ill. I've got 7 younger brothers and sisters which means that I'm in charge. I checked on my mum to see if she had woken up yet but she was asleep, lying peacefully and breathing steadily.

I decided to leave for school. I didn't have any breakfast because there wasn't any food at home. I had to run 3 miles to school and when I finally got there, I was just in time for registration. There are about 72 children in my class. We went to assembly and then had English. I am not bragging but I am the best in English. I was the first to finish so I raised my hand.

'Why are you not doing your work Ms Gray?'

'I've finished,' I said, 'and I would prefer if you'd call me by my first name which is Elizabeth.'

Big mistake! She was going to hit me with the cane …

Magdalene Nyadu (12)
Lord Lawson of Beamish School, Birtley

A Gun Attack In A Gun Shop

'What happened here?' Detective Collins asked the shopkeeper.

'Some maniac decided he would take a sub-machine gun and a can of spray paint to my shop, luckily it was closed,' the shopkeeper explained, 'but the gun wasn't from this shop, I only sell handguns and rifles for home security, guns like that aren't available legally.'

'So what are you saying, Mr Kolaska, the gun is illegal?' Collins added.

'Bingo!'

'Thanks for your help, Mr Kolaska. If you think of anything else here's my card,' Collins said.

Back in the lab, 18 different sets of fingerprints were found but all of them were belonging to customers that had been and gone from the shop without causing any disruption.

Collins decided to go back and check for any evidence missed the first time round.

'Can I have a look at your stock order form, Mr Kolaska, that is if you don't mind?' Collins asked, expecting a positive response.

'Actually, detective, I *do* mind. Do you have a warrant?' he replied.

'No, Sir, I do not have a warrant, but the law confirms that a detective automatically has the right to search a crime scene and/or witnesses and victims. So Mr Kolaska, your order form?' Collins stated, eager to know what Kolaska had to hide.

Unfortunately, Collins was no further forward. The answer didn't lie in the order form, but in the bullet. It was from a handgun, not a machine gun. Mr Kolaska's bank balance isn't particularly high but insurance in Vegas is.

Evan Hook (12)
Lord Lawson of Beamish School, Birtley

The Siege

5 weeks after the virus escaped, many people who we knew and loved had died due to the infection. Now only me, Kerry and Millen and of course Kerry's dog, Pedro, were left.

We were searching for a place safe from the virus.

'Derrek, where are we going?' Kerry asked again.

'As far south as possible,' I replied bitterly.

The virus had appeared in the north and slowly but steadily, crawled into England.

Millen was being unusually quiet.

'What's wrong Millen?' I spoke in a low-toned voice. He ignored me.

3 weeks later we made it to Dover. We found it more difficult to find food every day, Our pace had slowed but we still lumbered on. There were no boats, no ships, no transport to escape. We settled ourselves inside a nearby pub as night started to creep in and we quickly drifted off into a silent slumber.

Kerry's screams had woken me. I slowly rolled over and discovered that Millen was dead! His body lay under a wooden beam that hung down from the roof. Pedro went frantic at her cries and leapt from Kerry's arms and galloped away. Kerry chased after her dog, while I was left behind, weak due to starvation.

I lay in the same position for maybe 2 days without sleep or water. I'd known for hours that she wasn't coming back. I closed my eyes. I let wave after wave of darkness sweep over me. My mind went blank. I died.

Dean Garrett (14)
Lord Lawson of Beamish School, Birtley

Leave

There was a tapping on my wall, 'Leave this house, *now!*' it said.

At first I thought it was my brother but he was on the other side of me. Where was it coming from? Who was it? I lay, puzzled in the darkness of my room.

Suddenly it turned cold. I wrapped my bedding around me. The voice came again. 'Leave this house, *now!*' it said, this time louder, more angry.

I was scared but it was good that it didn't come again. I fell asleep for the rest of the night.

The same thing happened the next night and the next. I tried to find out where it came from. My back wall. Instead of tapping it was a scraping sound. Scratching, scraping at my wall. The thing is my back wall is the end of the house with no house attached to it. The walls aren't thick either so how was it here, coming from my wall I mean?

'Leave this house, *now!*'

'Why?' I asked. 'Why must I?'

'You will die! You and only you!'

'What have I done?'

'You hold the curse, the curse of death.'

'No I don't. You just want to scare me! I won't leave! I won't, I won't, I won't!'

'You shall suffer!'

Now I can't wake up. I wish I had listened, oh I so wish I had.

Sophie Fenwick (12)
Lord Lawson of Beamish School, Birtley

A Day In The Life Of Me

I wake up at around 7am but I don't get up till 7.30am. I then get ready for school. I get washed and have my breakfast and at 8am my friends come for me to walk to school.

At around 8.40am I arrive at school and wait till 8.45 for the hooter to go. I then go to tutorial and my tutor takes the register, tells us if there are any notices and sorts out any problems with uniform etc.

School finishes at 3.15pm and in a school day there are 6 lessons. There is also a break, which last 15 minutes, starting at 10am. There is also another break at 12.25 and that lasts 50 minutes.

At around 3.40pm I get in from school. I get changed straight away and go downstairs for my tea. At 5pm my friends come for me and we go and call on our other friends. I walk around for a couple of hours with my mates.

I go in between 9 and 9.30pm and watch TV for half an hour. Then go in the bath or shower. Depending on what time I come out the bath or shower, I then make a cup of tea or coffee and go and get ready for bed. When I finish the tea or coffee I go to bed and watch the TV, DVD or a video till I fall asleep.

Nicola Wray (14)
Lord Lawson of Beamish School, Birtley

A Day In The Life Of Jade Stobbart

This is a piece of writing about a typical day in my friend Jade's life …

Morning time

In the morning Jade gets up at 7.30am and goes to the bathroom to get washed and clean her teeth. After doing this she has her breakfast, usually toast.

At 8.10am she meets her friends Leanne and Stephanie at the shop and they get the bus to school.

When they arrive at school, Jade goes to Brookside. At 8.45am the hooter goes and she goes to tutorial, then morning lessons.

Lunchtime

At lunchtime Jade goes to the canteen with her friends, Nicola, Leanne, Stephanie and me. After eating she and Leanne go to Brookside for a chat with their other friends. They stay until the hooter goes, then they go to tutorial and last two lessons.

At home

After walking home, Jade picks her sister up from her school. She then goes home to get changed. She has her tea then calls for Leanne. The both of them go to James' to go on his trampoline and have fun. She goes back home at 9.30pm.

Night-time

When she comes in she goes in the bath and cleanses her face. She then has her supper. At 10pm she goes upstairs to listen to music. At 10.30pm she gets into bed and reads her book. Then, watching 'Gimme, Gimme, Gimme', she falls asleep and waits for her next day to begin.

Kirsty White (14)
Lord Lawson of Beamish School, Birtley

The Siege

Yesterday, 30 children were released after a 3-week siege.

Scientists noticed this deadly, contagious disease and immediately warned the school. They later realised that only one room in the whole school was affected.

Everyone was evacuated, bar that class. They had to remain in the room for 3 weeks.

Each child was allowed a carrier bag each of their personal possessions, but at the end of the 3 weeks, everything had to be burnt.

Most of the children just had things like magazines, deodorant, shampoo, make-up etc, things that they wouldn't really mind being burnt.

All the class came up with 5 rules for the 3 weeks they would be in there:
* No violence.
* Remember safety.
*Tidy up after yourself.
*Always be polite and thoughtful.
*Don't take too much food.

They also came up with a rota to share time and things. Breakfast would be between 8am-9am, dinner at 12pm-1pm and tea at 4pm-5pm.

Only 2 electrical appliances could be picked on top of the microwave they had already been given. They chose a TV and a camping cooker.

They rearranged the classroom so that it was better. They put all the tables around the outside. One of the rooms was changed into a toilet and changing area.

Children also entertained themselves by graffitiing the walls, reading, drawing, socialising or using other items from their carrier bags.

These children have been traumatised. This is an experience they will not forget.

Leanne Tiffen (14)
Lord Lawson of Beamish School, Birtley

Gantz

A short young boy stood at the station, absorbed by the comic he was reading. His neck leant to one side, letting his dark black hair hang down.

Langholm Station was buzzing with people as the trains had been delayed. A small old lady walked up to the boy. She didn't seem to have a sense of balance as she swayed very noticeably. 'Ex ... excuse me, may I ask you a question?'

The boy glared down at the lady. He really couldn't be bothered to speak to some random hag.

'Can I get to Hinode Station from here?'

'Yeah, you can,' he lied.

'I see. Thank you very much.' She shuffled off into the crowd of people as he continued reading.

A while later the old lady came back, slightly disappointed. 'Pardon me again, I don't think this is the right place after all ...'

The boy ground his teeth and turned his head towards her, 'Look, lady, try to figure it out on your own, yeah? Don't rely on other people so much.'

The old lady nodded and walked away. 'I'm sorry ...'

God, the old are so stupid he thought to himself. *Even worse than the young who are absolute crap for brains, I swear.*

Another boy walked up beside him. He was tall, slender and well-dressed. A man wearing a thick coat and holding a half-drunk beer bottle in his left hand stumbled out of the crowd of people and fell onto the railway lines.

'Oww ...'

People started mumbling and commotion started in the mass of people.

That guy's way plastered. No station attendants are coming ... no one will come down to help him, not a guy like that. The short boy wouldn't care much if the man died, he didn't know him and besides, it's not often you get to see a man die.

The tall boy's clasped hands were shaking and sweat rolled down his face. He clenched his eyes shut and said to himself, 'Okay, I'll do it.' He hopped down onto the train tracks and ran over to the man had fallenl.

Crap it's him, what's he doing? He's going to die! What a moron, is he trying to show off? Thoughts flashed through the boy's head like lightning flashes as he watched his childhood friend attempt to pick up the man.

'Hey somebody, get down and help!' the tall boy shouted, pleaded for help yet nobody came down, all too terrified to risk their lives for some drunk. The tall boy looked around, his sweat dripping off his chin onto the tracks. He glanced at a boy with a comic book in his hand. 'Keenan! Is that you Keenan?'

Oh God, absolutely not. Don't look at me that way people, you go instead! No, why am I climbing down? Why am I risking my life for that stupid bum? Am I happy he recognised me or something?

A loud, muffled voice echoed across the area. 'Train now arriving on line 2. Please step back behind the white line.'

A look of shock tore through the boys' faces, they were stunned momentarily. Shouts from the crowd begging for them to hurry flew past their ears. The tall boy quickly dragged the man up onto the platform. Groups of people were shouting to run. The two of them half ran, half stumbled along the track then a woman shouted, 'What's the point of running from a train? Get up!'

The two of them stopped in a paralysed state, unable to move, when they heard this.

'Keep running!' the tall boy shouted, there was no time to think about what to do so they ran for their lives, getting chased by the train, then it hit them. Their bodies flew across the track and the terrified looks on people's faces went across the platform. *Bzzt.*

The two of them were in a small, square, wooden room panting like enraged dogs. There were other people and a dog in the corner, all huddled up against each other. A small man with glasses stood up. 'Were you boys about to die too?'

Keenan stared at the strange situation. The only thing he could tell was he was never going to go back.

Alex Duckett-Pike (14)
Lord Lawson of Beamish School, Birtley

Under Siege

One day in an English classroom, everything was going fine until one of the pupils threw up, *a lot.* An ambulance was called and an armoured car arrived. Two men stepped out, fully geared in *Hazmat* suits and wielding a Geiger counter.

The instant the counter entered the classroom, the needle went ballistic. The two men nodded. One addressed the class. 'One or more of you have contracted the Velvet Death, named for its colour and its prolonged results. The area is now under quarantine and will be for the next fortnight and a half. We apologise for the inconvenience.' He walked out and men began setting up an air-tight tent scarily quick around all orifices that particles might escape through.

'Hey! If only one or more of us is infected, why do the rest of us have to stay?' a panicky girl asked.

'Because we don't know how many or *which* of you *are* infected!' He stepped out of the room, before it was sealed. His head reappeared (still helmeted) through an air passage box in the tent's wall. 'Follow orders and you will get out of this alive and well.'

'Yeah, you can say that from *that* side of the tent!'

'Don't worry,' the *Hazmat* man said, 'all the necessary preparations are being made. You'll be like one, big, happy family!'

The class looked at each other uneasily. *Of course we will*, I thought sarcastically.

Alex Stoker (14)
Lord Lawson of Beamish School, Birtley

Siege Strikes Secondary School

An amazing, mysterious disease is rapidly slicing through a secondary school in the north-east of England. Lord Lawson of Beamish School in Birtley has been struck by this obscure, deadly disease.

Many children have had to be kept in their classrooms for a matter of days now.

Not knowing how long the children will be there, special design scientists have installed a boiler and a microwave in the classroom so the children have access to fresh water and they can have hot meals, also brought to them by the scientists.

'The children can't feel the disease until they get touched by a surface. When that occurs they are left in searing pain and *golf ball like* blood blisters appear on the body', Dr Brownsmith explained. 'Once the children have the disease it is incurable and they will have it for the rest of their lives'.

The children's parents have been fully informed of these details regarding their children and the scientists are doing the best they can to stop the spread of the disease.

When all the children come out of school, the whole school will have to be burnt down, which will mean any clothes, bags and personal items will be lost.

Thomas Sproates (13)
Lord Lawson of Beamish School, Birtley

A Day In The Life Of A Siege Pupil

I woke up early this morning, no one else was awake. The siege is boring now, it was OK at first. It has only been five days so far and I'm stressed already. We're only stuck in here because a boy caught a disease and it was contagious. Everyone else was beginning to catch it so we have to be locked in this class for three weeks, until the disease clears. Nightmare!

Resources will be passed through the window by men wearing special suits. A tap is being installed through the outer wall with fresh running water. We only have a microwave to cook food in.

Before and after each meal we have to get all the tables out then put them all away, then get them back out. It's such a fuss.

After breakfast I queued for the wash and change room. Eventually I washed and changed, it was freezing in the room, it was damp.

At tea today one boy kept being sick all over, it smelt like a human had been locked in a room for days without getting washed, not someone's sick.

The first few days in here have been exciting, staying in a class, not doing any school work, but now it's boring, the days drag on.

It's late night, everyone's asleep. I'm always the last to go to bed and first to wake up. I'm missing my family and friends. Going to bed now.

Shauna Service (14)
Lord Lawson of Beamish School, Birtley

Quarantine?

The world's top scientists were all sitting in a small room, surrounding a table.

'We have no choice,' one of them said, 'quarantine is the only answer.'

'They're only kids for God's sake,' another shouted, 'we can't put them in isolation!' He had a point.

The government weren't going to let them lock a group of fourteen-year-old children in a school classroom.

'Look,' a third yelled, 'this is an incredibly deadly disease. Exactly how deadly we are not sure, but we do know that we cannot release this upon the world.'

There was a short tap on the door.

'Enter,' one scientist said.

A short woman walked in carrying a large pile of papers.

'What is it?' the scientists asked.

'Sir, the test results have come back from the laboratory. They have been able to figure out exactly what the disease does from blood samples taken from the children.'

'Well what are you waiting for? Bring them here at once.'

The second scientist stood up again. 'I don't care what they say, we cannot put a group of teenagers into quarantine!'

'Just sit down and shut up! We will wait until we have read this before we make any rash decisions.' He picked up the papers and started to read through them. As he finished, his eyes widened and he dropped back down into his seat, stunned. Then in a squeaky, high-pitched, frightened voice he murmured, 'We have no choice. Quarantine *is* the only answer ...'

Daniel Norton (14)
Lord Lawson of Beamish School, Birtley

Disease Hits Children

Today I woke up on the fifth day in this dull, dreadful, diseased place. I don't feel good. I'm tired and hungry and bored out of my mind because I'm trapped in this small, dingy place for three weeks. I don't think I can last any longer. I didn't bring any good or special items with me because at the end of this diseased three weeks the scientists are going to burn everything that we've brought and everything we've worn, so instead of bringing special things I just brought some junk food, playing cards, disposable toothbrush with toothpaste and roll-on deodorant, to get me through this time.

Later on in the day me, Jamie and Ryan played cards. This was a typical day in the English room. Then after that we had our breakfast and then watched TV for three hours. This brought the time to twelve o'clock and by this time it was dinner time. We had sausages and mashed potatoes which the scientists brought in through the window. After that we all sat down and watched the film, 'Lord of the Rings' which one of the pupils brought in and after that had finished I could tell that people were bored and tired because everyone started to get restless. After all of that we had to go back to bed.

In the morning I'll have to do exactly the same thing again, for two more weeks. I'm not looking forward to that.

Marc Lonsdale (14)
Lord Lawson of Beamish School, Birtley

The Girl Who Lost Her Puppy

Once upon a time there was a little girl called Faye who had a puppy called Lauren. Lauren was quite a scruffy-looking puppy, she only had three legs, one ear and no fur, except a very distinguishing ring of fur around her belly. Lauren might have been scruffy but she was a lovely little dog, just like her owner Faye.

Faye had bright red, curly hair, she was always dressed in lovely pink dresses, she also always had pink flower clips in her hair to keep it off her face so that everyone could see her blinding smile.

Faye often took Lauren out for walks in the nearby forest and Lauren behaved really well. This was the main reason Faye took her because she behaved so well and she wanted to treat her. Taking Lauren into the forest made Faye happy but Faye was always happy anyway, she was forever giggling and bounding around.

You may be thinking that it was a perfect life for Lauren, having such a lovely owner like Faye, despite the fact she only had three legs, one ear and no fur. You will probably be asking yourself how Lauren got into such a mess. Well here's how it happened …

Lauren was knocked over by an eighteen-wheel truck and lost a leg, an ear and her fur. Oh and her tail! Lauren from there was placed in a dog shelter, but Lauren didn't like being cooped up in a cage all day. So when it was time for tea and they were let out to go to the doggy dining room, she ran and ran and ran as fast as her three legs could carry her. She was running quite fast, considering she only had three legs.

This was where she met Faye, who took her in and cared for her. Faye could never have been happier, her dream had finally come true. This was having a puppy. Although Lauren had a bad past, she was a very cheerful dog which was exactly the same as Faye. Faye and Lauren were two of a kind! Faye put up with nasty comments being snarled at Lauren, by saying, 'Well if you look like that without being hit by a truck, I'd hate to think what you'd look like if you were hit by one!'

After having Lauren for three months, Faye took her out into the forest for her usual walk as she had been a good puppy, but as Faye and Lauren entered the forest, Lauren tried to get off her lead so Faye let her off but before she could say, 'Fetch that stick,' Lauren was off. Faye chased after her but Lauren, once again, ran and ran and ran as fast as her three little legs could carry her, so fast Faye had to stop. It was no use, Lauren was gone again!

Holly Coates (14)
Lord Lawson of Beamish School, Birtley

Untitled

(An extract)

In a desperate attempt to beat Akito and to keep up his honour as a fighter, Akuryou didn't care what it took to become the strongest, most fearsome fighter. This strong desire, this need for power, to give everything he had just for the strength to beat Akito, unlocked the true origin of his powers and full potential of his demon god side, making him a true demigod, an angel of darkness, chaos … death … However, this power was too strong for his own mind, it became clouded in darkness … his soul corrupted by the powers of evil he wielded. For two and a half long years after the fight against Akito, no one ever saw Akuryou again … but things changed rapidly after that …

'This is Maxwell Grant, for ICO News. The event that just took place here, not even the eyewitnesses who saw what happened could believe it, it's a huge disaster … and God knows how many lives this may have cost and … hmm, just received news that some people claim to have seen a black-winged angel just before the explosion happened. My opinion is this; probably just drunk people, or the usual crazed people who claim to have seen something unexplained … who mistake a crow or another black bird for this.

It's a real tragedy people, it seems that a large part of New York has been destroyed … another attack by terrorists? A new weapon they crea - … what's this? There's something hovering in the sky.'

The camera turned away from the reporter and pointed up to the sky. It was hard to see but whatever it was it did have huge wings. The camera turned back to the news reporter.

'This, it must just be the bird they mistook … for … hmm, what's this?' The reporter ducked and disappeared from the TV screen.

The news show was seen on every TV channel. The camera followed soon enough, showing the reporter picking up a large black feather which had just dropped to the ground. He looked at it and back at the camera. 'I don't know what's going on, but this … is sure no ordinary bird, I - … argh!'

The screen flashed white for a second. When it returned to normal, the camera lay on its side, blood could be seen on the ground, people could be heard screaming, there was a loud rumbling noise in the background coming from explosions. The sky turned dark and so did the TV screen …

Liam Archer (14)
Lord Lawson of Beamish School, Birtley

School Children Free

Finally school children of Year 9, English Set 3, of Lord Lawson of Beamish School have been set free after spending three weeks in isolation.

The children had been isolated in the same classroom because of an outbreak of a contagious disease called Lawson's Fever. The scientists are fairly certain that the disease has not spread, but if you or anyone you know are experiencing a yellow rash on the back of the neck and legs, then please contact your GP. The whole of Birtley Town will be vaccinated against this deadly disease within a few weeks and leaflets will be handed out shortly.

If you have any questions, then please ring our hotline on: 1234765.

Reported by Matthew Kennedy, 12th October 2007.

Matthew Kennedy (14)
Lord Lawson of Beamish School, Birtley

Disease Strikes School!

This week, a highly contagious and deadly disease has been spread throughout a school in Birtley. The school, named Lord Lawson of Beamish, has had to keep ten pupils in for a minimum of three weeks.

Throughout the three weeks, the children will receive clean clothes every three days, however they'll get clean underwear every day.

Yesterday we got the names of the ten pupils that will be staying in the school. The pupils are: Ben Robinson, Matthew Kennedy, Kenneth Johnstone, Steven Richardson, Laura Paxton, Matthew Lloyd, Shawn Mayall, Kieran Martin, David Newby and Ryan Jenkins.

We spoke to the headmaster and he had this to say. 'We understand the controversy that this has caused, however we feel that this is necessary so that the disease does not get passed through the area'.

Parents of the children that have to stay in school are worried, but they understand that it does have to be done.

More on this issue tomorrow.

Ryan Jenkins (14)
Lord Lawson of Beamish School, Birtley

A Day In The Life Of A Siege Student

I woke up at 8 o'clock and was lying in bed wondering what the day would bring. Eventually I got up and got in the queue for the washroom. I was still half asleep, but managed to keep myself standing. I was there for a while. Eventually I got to the front of the queue, got washed and dressed and came out. That woke me up a bit. As I headed across the room towards my area, Mrs Morton stopped me and asked how I was feeling. I just said not too good and walked away before she could say anything else. A disease had spread through my class and we had to stay in our classroom for three weeks.

The only thing that kept me going was the thought of Chris, the nicest lad in my school, being in the same room. After I got back it was nearly lunchtime. A voice said, 'Lunch.' I got up and went over; beans on toast again. I went to find a seat. Some friends were already sitting there so I joined them. After a while I had to go and do the washing up as it was my turn.

After that there was nothing to do until teatime. I spent that time texting my friends. Teatime was the same as dinner time, except it was a cheese toasty. Then the night came, I spent the night talking to Chris. I'd never actually talked to him like this before, he was so nice. After that I went to bed and dreamt about him.

Sophie Hood (14)
Lord Lawson of Beamish School, Birtley

Stranded

There they were, standing on the edge of death at the top of the tallest mountain ever recorded, Mount Camata. The two explorers, Jack and Rachel, were standing stranded on this natural wonder, with no supplies or equipment to get to the bottom safely.

It all started when they were flying to their base camp after searching the hidden temple of the Aztecs a few days earlier, when their group leader stunned them by throwing them out of the plane with nothing to help them - not even parachutes. It was a miracle that they'd even survived the great fall of a thousand feet. They were stranded and they could not do anything.

After a few hours of lying unconscious on the grass verge right at the top of the great mountain, they slowly woke up. They both were confused about the events that had taken place, they didn't know how they got there. After looking around Rachel said, 'I think that ... James threw us out of the plane, that's how we are here, stranded with nothing to save us!'

'Maybe he wanted the Aztec treasures and artefacts for himself. He always was selfish,' Jack replied.

Rachel shuddered and then said, amazed, 'But how did we survive the fall without any support or parachutes?'

Jack stood for a while, thinking. After a few seconds he whispered to himself, 'We escaped the falling rocks in the temple without being harmed, and then we fell thousands of feet to the top of here, but still survived when we really should have died.' He then put his hand in his hunting jacket and pulled it back out. He was holding an Aztec coin; he looked surprised. 'Rachel, Rachel, I now how we survived the fall ... I found this coin in my pocket, it's from the hidden temple. It must have fallen into my pocket when we were collecting the treasure. That's what it is, it must be lucky or something.'

Rachel reached over with astonishment. 'It can't be that, it just can't be, it's not possible.'

'It must be, that's all that can explain it,' Jack answered. 'I will test it. I'll jump of this edge and if I land on that platform down there, then it *is* what I think,' Jack announced.

Rachel shouted, 'That must be about a hundred feet down there, if it doesn't work, then you will die.' She then walked away and started to cry.

'I know it is dangerous, but I am sure that it will work. If it doesn't I have to say this to you ... it doesn't matter. Just forget I ever said that it will work, don't worry, it w-will,' Jack stuttered ...

Adam Wilkinson (14)
Lord Lawson of Beamish School, Birtley

Untitled

The music was bouncing around in my head. Will Smith was blaring out from the speakers. We were at the village nightclub and it was almost finished. I had told Dad that Jenn was taking me home, but really I was walking home. My dad would kill me if he knew, especially as I was walking alone. 'Amarillo' had just finished and that was the cue to leave.

It was light when we had got to the club, but now it was very dark. It was as if a blanket had been laid over the world and it had become night. The bitter wind whirled around me as I waved my friends goodbye. I was freezing in my short skirt and strapless top; it was then I realised I should have taken the offer of a lift.

I started walking down the cut; it seemed even darker down there. I started walking, looking over my shoulder anxiously. I was scared!

I walked further down the path and as I did, it felt as if icy cold fingers were scratching at the back of my neck. It was then that I heard light footsteps. I turned around. No one was there. I carried on walking. The trees' branches were like fingers, scratching away at me. I was breathing heavily. I was scared. Why didn't I take the offer of the lift? Why?

The footsteps started again. They were getting quicker and quicker, faster and faster. I looked behind frantically; no one was there. I was walking past the old graveyard now. I remembered the days Jenn and I used to spend playing in the long grass with the angel statues watching over us. We felt safe then. The angels seemed to have turned into devils, poking their sticks at me. I realised then I wasn't safe.

I carried on walking, faster and faster, quicker and quicker. The footsteps were doing the same. I could hear heavy breathing, it was warm and tickling the back of my neck. I looked behind. I saw a shadow jumping into the nearest bush. I was scared, very scared. It felt as if my heart was ready to pound out of my body. I started running faster and faster, quicker and quicker. The stranger was running too. The stranger's shadow was on the ground from the reflection of the moon. I saw my house; it seemed to be getting further away. The shadow drew something out of its pocket. I ran, my house became nearer.

So close, but yet so far …

Lauren Rutherford (14)
Lord Lawson of Beamish School, Birtley

Untitled

(An extract)

Bang!

'Run, Johnny, run!'

Johnny hurtled through the ash and smoke.

'Almost there, Johnny, come on, come on!' All I could do was yell and hope he could hear me. I could see a black figure bursting through the sparks towards my position. An enemy plane circled above, watching, waiting. It loomed above like a storm waiting for the precise moment to strike its lightning.

Johnny was barely 10 metres away from me when the escape vehicle disappeared through the smog. When Johnny reached me, I collapsed into a struggling spasm of emotions. I was scared, angry and mortified. Our own men, some of whom I had personally saved, had left us in the middle of a war zone. How would I know if we would make it out alive?

We were the new army recruits, I was Special Officer Eric Barns and I was with my colleague, Jonathan (Johnny) Campbell. We were in Iraq trying to recover some documents stolen from Camp 73. We took the documents back, but were caught fleeing the scene …

There was ash everywhere, like a sea of black sand. We crawled through it and found an old rusty bunker. It was cramped, damp and derelict. We climbed into it and tried to salvage as much as we could. There was a rifle, empty bean can and a parachute. Without thinking, Johnny shoved these into his backpack. We had no plan, but we had to survive.

I awoke staring at a pair of vast black boots standing inside the bunker in front of me. I swallowed hard and held my breath. I feared the worst. Suddenly, I felt a sharp thump on the back of my head and I went out like a light.

I woke with a start to realise my clothes had gone. I looked around, but couldn't see Johnny anywhere. I was in a small, damp cage, I felt like an animal. It smelt really bad and I realised the enemy had found us. I daren't shout, as the guards had machetes. I looked through the icy bars of my cage. I gazed around to see the prisoners I'd seen on the ITN news; they were shouting at me. I shut my eyes …

Alex Kirton (14)
Lord Lawson of Beamish School, Birtley

The Siege Escape

It was a normal day at Fullerfield School, when all of a sudden, some scientists locked one of the school's Year 9 classes in their English classroom. Whilst doing this, the scientists planted a bug and a camera in the room. The scientists called it 'The Bug Project'. The doors were locked and it had started, 'The Siege'. Some of the children tried to get out, but everything was sealed shut. All of the children and the teacher all tried to get out, but it was useless.

After a couple of days the scientists noticed a decline in the teacher, Mr Christian Kane's health. After 12 hours he was dead. The children were ordered not to touch the body, and the smell of the corpse was horrendous.

The next day a child got ill and then died. This happened again and again over the next few days, until there was only one child left, Drew. Drew was removed from the room and put into an isolation booth, as the scientists wanted to do experiments on him to see why he hadn't got the disease. It turned out that Drew wasn't human.

The police found out about what the scientists had done and then arrested them all. The police never found Drew or one other scientist.

The scientist was called Evan. Evan took Drew and travelled around the world doing lots of experiments on him, and then six months later, Drew *escaped* …

Christina Bailey (13)
Lord Lawson of Beamish School, Birtley

It ...

It was a dark, cold morning in the darkness of the moist grey forest. As I started to walk deeper into the darkness of the trees, I came to a terrifying stop. Standing tall in front of me loomed a dark cave. On the outside of the cave there were patterns, hundreds of them. In the far left corner of my eye, I could see a hole in the cave. Then from the darkness of the cave crept out something, someone, with a sheet spread across its arms in the shape of a human body, blood dripping, making a train along the floor. As it walked over to the hole, it threw the body down into the hole.

My senses were telling me not to go any further, but I did. I walked over to the hole. I looked down. All I could see was this white bundle mixed with red blood on the floor. I had so many thoughts running through my head. Then I remembered what my grandfather had told me. The story was about the beast that captured innocent people and removed their vital organs to replace its own with theirs.

I heard the leaves crackle behind me. I turned round. There it was in front of me. Its eyes were glistening with pain and fury. I made a run for it through the forest. I ignored its cries and just ran. I got into my car and sped off. I was safe ... for now.

Glen McLeod (14)
Lord Lawson of Beamish School, Birtley

The Meteor!

It was 2035 and the world was becoming desperately short of fossil fuels and oil had totally run out. The world was becoming desperate and many people wished they had done something about the environment sooner. The Russian space port discovered a giant rock the size of California was heading for Earth and would impact in four days.

The meteor that was called Mecta, hit the Earth in the south of Germany. It killed thousands and caused a 300-foot cavity. Scientists from all over the world analysed the meteor which Ryan author, the best British scientist, discovered that it had a new element he called 'authanium' that could be renewed, and it was much like a fossil fuel they most desperately need.

The American government tested the new product in missiles; they found that it was very effective in destroying every electronic component in a certain radius. The new bomb was sent to every major country in the world. Just after they were place, the missiles started firing at each other and multiplying into everyday objects and destroyed them, causing the world serious problems.

Ryan created a device called the Anti-Authanium Activator which destroyed the entire product, except the ones used as a natural resource. Once the world had gone back to normal, all the world leaders gathered to sign a contact to never use authanium as a weapon of war. Although it was still used as a resource and because of this, the world could carry on using this product without being in fear that it would one day run out.

Steven Hudspith (14)
Lord Lawson of Beamish School, Birtley

A Day In The Life Of Me

A day in the life of me starts at 7am in the morning, when my alarm clock goes off. I dread the sound because I know I have to get up, or I will be late.

I go downstairs for my breakfast. Normally I have a bit of toast. I don't normally feel hungry, but my mam makes me have breakfast to get my energy levels up and keep me going till dinnertime.

Every morning I try and aim to finish my breakfast at around 7.15am. Then I go upstairs and do all the stuff, like get washed, brush my teeth, then comes the dreaded part of doing my hair and make-up. This is when I should not be disturbed, as I do get stressed as some mornings my make-up won't go right. The worst part is when I have a BHD (bad hair day). This is what every girl dreads to think of. After my stress levels have gone down, I get dressed then walk to school at 8.30am.

I go and see my friends and tell them all the gossip that has happened the night before. Then by the time we all have finished our gossip, the bell goes for lessons.

There is nothing much to tell you about the lessons as I don't listen to half of it. (Don't tell the teachers though.) Then the best time of the day comes, quarter past three. I love that time because I can go home, and that's a day less until the weekend.

Rachel Hall (14)
Lord Lawson of Beamish School, Birtley

A Day In The Life Of Smokey (My Cat)

Ah! That was a good night's sleep. Can always rely on Jayde's alarm clock to wake me up just in time for breakfast.

Yum! That was delicious! My mum gets the best chicken Felix. I'm still a bit hungry, I think I might go outside and see if I can catch a bird.

Oh, I can see one there, eating worms. I feel a bit guilty, the bird has done nothing to me and I'm just going to eat it! Oh well, a cat's gotta eat! Excuse me for a minute! Um, ah, get here you little … OK, I'm back, I got it. I'm going back inside now, coming?

I feel all muddy now, I think I need a wash. (Sometime later!) 'Cough, cough.' Sorry, hairball! I think I'm going to find a warm spot on Jayde's bed and close my eyes, cos you know I do need my rest! I'm getting old as well!

Uh-oh, what's that? Oh no, it's that sucking machine again! Better go and hide somewhere! Oh that basket of clothes looks safe and warm. Oh, this is lovely and warm. Jayde calls that evil cat-sucking machine a Hoover! The only thing that thing hoovers is my tail!

Yes! It's teatime at last! I wonder what Mum's given me this time? It's my favourite, beef Felix and Go-Kat biscuits! That was better than breakfast and the bird put together! I might go have a nap now! Today's been an adventure. Thanks for joining me! See ya!

Jayde Guy (13)
Lord Lawson of Beamish School, Birtley

Hold The Front Page

The recent scandal in Formula 1 came to a close today at a hearing in Paris in front of the FIA. The British American racing team (BAR) were found guilty of breaking weight restrictions at last weekend's San Marino GP. This meant that Jenson Button lost his third place and BAR's only points of the season. The rules state that the car must weigh 600 kilos, but the car weighed in at 594 kilos at the weigh-in after the race.

In front of the FIA, the BAR technical director said, 'Nowhere in the rules says that fuel can add up the extra weight, so we used it to our advantage. Now we have been punished for this'.

When the event came about, BAR were almost certain to be thrown out of this year's championship, but the weight breaking wasn't as severe as it was first thought to be because it wasn't broken by 10 kilos.

They will now miss the next two races in Spain and Monaco. Jenson Button had this to say, 'This could decide my future at this team, as I have an opportunity to move to Williams next season'.

This may well ruin BAR's entire season, as they have no points from four races. They are said to be starting next season's campaign plans now.

Simon Gray (14)
Lord Lawson of Beamish School, Birtley

A Day In The Life Of Me

My life is the same as any other 14-year-old girl, with some exceptions. It all starts at 7am when my alarm clock goes off and I get out of bed, slowly and quietly. I get dressed, do my hair and use the bathroom in less than half an hour. Not very many others can say that about themselves now, can they! After that, I go downstairs to have some breakfast and a cup of coffee to keep me awake during school. By the time 7.50am comes, I have left the house and will be on my way down to the bus stop to catch the bus.

When I'm at school I feel happy 'cause I know that I am surrounded by the people I love and who love me back. My group of Gothic friends are like my extended family; I have those who are my closest and I love dearly, then those I don't really like but put up with anyway, 'cause I have to. With my friends there are never two days that are the same, there are always new jokes and topics to talk about.

Now after school, I'm a totally different person. I have to come home and look after my niece, who takes a lot of my time and eats a considerable amount of food for the thin girl she is. Once she is fed and watered, I have to start to look after the house, but not for long as my mum comes in at about 6.30pm. Then I live my life and my weekends are crazy!

Samantha Florentine (14)
Lord Lawson of Beamish School, Birtley

The Idea That Shocked The Village

Little Bobbyns was a village bigger than its name. Everyone knew each other's business because not many people lived there. The events that would soon be happening in the village would shock even the most unshockable of residents.

On the east side of the village there stood a grand, proud house as old as its owner. That proud house belonged to William Barron, the mayor. He was a happy, bright soul who laughed at his own unfunny jokes. If you saw him, he would be smiling and laughing, even if there was nothing to smile or laugh about. That's just the way he was!

Wearing a cloak of periwinkle-blue, he rounded up the inhabitants into the village hall for a last minute meeting, which they often held. He chuckled at the unsuspecting villagers as they piled into the hall, racing for their particular seat, which they had to their liking. Grinning wider than a Cheshire cat, he followed behind them, along with his papers.

He took himself and his papers to the platform, where he would often begin to tell them why they were there. You could see their eyes popping out of their sockets, not because he was wearing a cloak, but because he shuffled through his papers loudly. The mayor was an eccentric man (often seen carrying a notebook and was never without a pen), who was forever trying to get the villagers to try new ideas. But his recent idea was absurd, *very absurd, unbelievable ...*

Abbi Fletcher (14)
Lord Lawson of Beamish School, Birtley

The Emperor's Daughter

Once upon a time there was a powerful emperor of China. He was tall with a grey beard that touched his knees.

Emperor Shinnyan had a beautiful daughter called Blossom; she had silky black hair. Everyone loved her, apart from the evil, selfish witch. There were pumpkins in the palace garden, which belonged to Blossom. The witch was jealous of her beauty, she poisoned all the pumpkins in the garden. Blossom ate one and was struck ill.

Emperor Shinnyan was taking one of his afternoon walks and found his daughter lying against the wishing well. He looked down the well and saw the little dragon, who informed the emperor that to make his daughter better, she needed to sip some unicorn's blood. However, the only way to attract a unicorn is the scent of a rare flower, which can only be found at the top of a mountain. The flower only blossoms every 155 years. There was someone who had a bottle of the scent, that person being the witch

Later on, the emperor went down the valley and stole the bottle of scent as the witch was out for lunch. The emperor spread the scent around the garden, and there before his eyes, a unicorn appeared. The emperor took some of the unicorn's blood by magic and gave it to his daughter. Blossom became well, and as he turned around, the unicorn had vanished. Blossom was never ill again.

Jared Davison (14)
Lord Lawson of Beamish School, Birtley

A Day In The Life Of Me

In my everyday life, I always wake up in the same place - my bedroom floor. For some strange reason, I always fall out of my bed in the middle of the night without realising it.

After I have woken up and untangled myself from my duvet, got ready, washed, I always go downstairs for my breakfast. As usual, I am the first one up as my mum and dad always sleep in.

Once I've had my breakfast, my older brother is usually up, and as usual, we start fighting, and this is when my mum and dad wake up to break up the fight. By this time, it's ten o'clock.

At ten o'clock I go and knock on my friend's door, we don't do a lot of anything in one day. We mostly play football for a few hours, have about an hour's rest, play football again for a few more hours, then go home for our tea. So then it is around five o'clock.

Five o'clock means hell - for my mum and dad it means more fighting between me and my brother, but this only lasts twenty minutes, as the tea is usually done. If we are having a Sunday dinner, as we sometimes do, the fighting continues - with food. We always start food fights. For some reason, it's always me who starts it - with beans! I use beans because my brother hates them, but then it's his fault, he shouldn't act like a jerk, trying to impress his friends when they come round.

At about five, I ring my friend if he is in. I go and knock on him, and yet again we play football, this time till about nine at night, that's when we go in. By then I'm exhausted and go to my bed and collapse in it, and the cycle starts again.

Dale Cowie (14)
Lord Lawson of Beamish School, Birtley

Myths And Legends

A long time ago, in the darkest corner of the Earth, laid a creature that was asleep for about 3,000 years. It was called the Minotaur. It was half man, half bull, which had caused destruction ever since the Egyptian times. It first appeared from the depths of the Roman Coliseum. Its chamber opened after the great fall of the stadium collapsing to the ground from a devastating earthquake. It escaped from the rubble and then thought that it should plan revenge on the people who'd locked it away in its prison.

First it planned to attack the Roman's country, Italy, because it was the place where they'd decided to lock it away for 3,000 years. It went up north to start the path of its destruction and nothing, not even the Romans, could stop the beast from attacking.

With its fury, it destroyed the Leaning Tower of Pisa, and then it flooded the whole town of Venice to its highest submerged level. It then intended to kill the Egyptian god, Osiris, who was the main person who locked it away in Rome for the whole time.

The stubborn beast swam across to Egypt to find the god who'd locked it away. With it, the beast destroyed the Great Pyramids of Egypt, along with the giant Sphinx. It found Osiris in the ancient city of Cairo. They decided that they'd fight for who'd get put away into the chamber underneath Rome. In the making of the decision, Osiris suddenly trapped the Minotaur and it was then locked away back underneath the Coliseum, never to be seen again.

Philip Campbell (14)
Lord Lawson of Beamish School, Birtley

The Figgymisgrugifooniyn

This is about the Figgymisgrugifooniyn, or Figgy for short. It is a creature that you should be warned about. If you see one, there are terrible consequences to that person if the Figgymisgrugifooniyn sees you and to any person that gets in their way.

The Figgymisgrugifooniyn may look cute, but is very deadly in fact. To identify one, you'll see a fuzzy, but very small creature that is about 20cm tall, with green, blue and orange patches all over its body.

When you see a Figgymisgrugifooniyn that is wet, you have to run in the opposite direction. Even if you are dying, you should run the other way, or drive if you're in a car. Once Figgymisgrugifooniyn gets wet, you're in big trouble because it turns into something terrifying and very, very ugly.

When the Figgymisgrugifooniyn gets wet, you'll see a very grotty and scraggly creature that is black from head to toe, and is about 15cm tall. It's very, very disgusting.

You have to make sure you run away, because when the Figgymisgrugifooniyn gets wet, it doesn't eat food like bread or bananas, it eats humans, cats and dogs. The Figgymisgrugifooniyn also gets bigger in size, depending on how many cats, dogs and people it has devoured.

When it's dry, it eats things like bananas and apricots as it is a herbivore, but when it transforms into the ugly Figgymisgrugifooniyn, it's a full-on carnivore. That's why you have to run in the opposite direction if you see it in its evil state.

A Figgymisgrugifooniyn will also destroy anything that gets in its way, like wood, metal, plastic and electronic devices. The only way to stop a Figgymisgrugifooniyn is either to shoot them or burn them to death. It's quite easy to kill them if you have a gun, or a flaming piece of wood lying around.

You've been warned!

Samantha Birleson (13)
Lord Lawson of Beamish School, Birtley

A Day In The Life Of A Siege Student

9.48am, I woke up. It was time for breakfast. It had already been passed through the window, the only interaction with us and the outside world. You see, a boy in our class had come down with a deadly virus and everyone had to be kept in quarantine for three weeks. We had been in for five days and already I couldn't stand it!

Anyway, breakfast, it was porridge. You see that was the only thing we could have breakfast-wise, we only had a microwave.

10.48am, I had read a book, talked to some people and slept a bit more. We had decided to have a game of hangman to pass the time. Clue: famous footballer, two words, five letters in the first and seven in the second.

Dinner time, microwave shepherds pie; surprise, surprise as always. So far, to pass the time before I got tired, I had got changed in the cupboard we were using as a changing room, and I'd washed from the cold tap that ran from the outside of the wall to us inside. There wasn't much else to do in our English classroom.

This had been a quiet day with nothing much happening. The only exciting thing was the boy that had started the illness off seemed to be getting better. That was great news. We all started to think maybe we would be out earlier than we thought.

Bedtime, we had to set the 'beds' out, which were really just bags as pillows and our coats, if we'd brought them, as blankets.

10.30pm, it's now bedtime in the day of a siege student.

Alice Suthren (14)
Lord Lawson of Beamish School, Birtley

A Quiet Day

It was a quiet day, the sun was shining, the birds were in their nests eating their lunch.

'Tweet, tweet,' went the birds. The birds had worms. They felt very happy it was such a beautiful day.

The wind was making a gentle breeze. The trees blew back and forth. The plants had grown so tall, they had beautiful roots and shiny leaves. The grass was blowing too.

Bethaney Goss (11)
Margaret Sutton School (Moderate Learning Difficulties), South Shields

The Magic Instrument

One day I was in the forest. I saw a magic instrument dancing around, then another instrument came out of the trees. Then the music was silent and smooth. It was a lovely instrument, it played a lovely tune. It kept on stopping and taking a break, kept on doing the same thing all the time.

The magic instrument was keeping me calm, until I heard a loud noise of the wind. I jumped, because the wind was getting wild and a little bit scary and I started to cry. So did the magic instrument, which was a flute.

The magic instrument came over to me and said, 'Are you alright?'

I said, 'I am fine.'

The magic flute guided me out of the forest and took me home to my mam and dad.

Kayleigh Davison (12)
Margaret Sutton School (Moderate Learning Difficulties), South Shields

Silver Coins Sparkling In The Sky Above

I was the first person in space and the first person to reach the silver sparkling stars. It was so magical and wonderful to reach the silver coins (the stars). When I was in space I was flying around like a wonderful, beautiful butterfly.

My ship landed on a star called Saturn. It was so real, so wonderful, so dreamy.

When I reached back to Earth I was 72 years old. I told my whole family everything - they were so pleased. For the rest of my life I just kept thinking about that wonderful time.

Let me tell you the story about the sparkling silver coins. The silver coins were planets - wonderful, dreamy planets - thousands sparkling in the dark sky. The planet Saturn was quiet with no one to disturb you. Before I went to space I was twelve years old. I ate food from my ship and there was just me and my mum on planet Saturn.

It took 25 years to get to Saturn. My mum died because we were there for 40 years. I was crying and just wanted to get back to Earth because I missed my family and friends.

So that's the story of the silver sparkling stars.

Adam Higginson (12)
Margaret Sutton School (Moderate Learning Difficulties), South Shields

My First Love

I was working in the park. She looked like an angel, 'my first love'. She was singing.

I started to cry. She looked at me and she was still singing. Again I just cried. She sounded so good. She was still singing and I just kept on crying. I gave her a watch and then I fell in love with my first love.

She sounded like something so sweet. People arrived, everyone cried so she stopped and she ran off and I was left alone.

Nathan Pallister (11)
Margaret Sutton School (Moderate Learning Difficulties), South Shields

Lonely And Sad

One night I sat by a window with a robin singing a song. I was lonely. A rabbit came towards me. I said hello. I gave it some milk. It sat on my knee. In the end the animals were my friends.

The animals came to me every day and I gave them milk. The animals made me happy and I was never lonely again.

Catherine Jones (12)
Margaret Sutton School (Moderate Learning Difficulties), South Shields

A Day In The Life Of A Pen

The pen once remembered being concealed in tight, shiny plastic surrounded by other hard blue pens. The pens would lie still on the shelf, while a wide variety of great shiny circles would stare at them - blue circles, brown circles, even green circles, big and small circles. The aliens would pick up the shiny plastic, then throw them back on the shelf.

Now the pen lay in a great huge block, this time surrounded by huge colourful sticks and a long, narrow, clear twig. Every now and then the pen would be roughly pulled out of the colourful block, sweaty hands would be wrapped around it. They would put the pen to paper and use the pen's fuel.

On the horrible days the pen would be thrown across the room to some other sweaty alien. Sometimes it would even be thrown into a deep dark hole. The deep dark hole would be thrown into a huge cylinder, where a sticky green solution would be poured all over. Then a great sea would flow into the cylinder and swish around.

Eventually when it was all over a great circle would be opened at the other end of the cylinder. And the pen would be thrown roughly into a huge silver hole where it was surrounded by empty yoghurt pots and bits of dirty paper.

Hannah Gray (12)
Our Lady & St Bede RC School, Stockton-on-Tees

A Day In The Life Of Thierry Henry

Ring, ring - the sound of the alarm clock wakes Thierry Henry up at 7am. He then slowly gets out of his four-poster bed and headed for the shower. He stepped out of the shower and wrapped himself in his warm, fluffy towel. He collected his bag and made his way to the Gunners' training ground. He gently slipped into his Subaru WRX and he drove off.

He got to the training ground and moved over to the changing rooms. He pulled on his bright white Nike Mercuria Vapor football boots and moved onto the pitch.

In the training session Thierry did running, passing and shooting drills. He then went for a shower and drove off to his mansion.

Later that day Thierry went to dinner with his manager Arsene Wenger and discussed a possible place into Europe and about tactics on how to win the FA Cup, which they were playing Manchester United for on Saturday.

Thierry got back late that night and he went straight to bed. He had had a busy day.

Robbie Stockburn (13)
Our Lady & St Bede RC School, Stockton-on-Tees

A Day In The Life Of Matthew

As the sun slowly rises I bring myself to wake up and enjoy the bliss of lying comfortably in my bed. As I get up I enjoy playing my guitar for ten long, relaxing minutes and play my favourite songs then get dressed in my ugly school uniform and go downstairs to eat my breakfast.

As I walk to school I enjoy the company of my friend Christopher and talk. School slowly creeps by. I walk home and go and see my friend Sean. We play an interesting game of soccer. I go home, eat my tasty tea and enjoy a cup of fruit juice and watch television and wait until my pudding, always mother's special. Then I enjoy playing my guitar again. Shortly after it's time to go to sleep. I lie in bed, curtains open and I relax. Slowly I drift off to sleep, then the day ends.

Matthew Sedgewick (13)
Our Lady & St Bede RC School, Stockton-on-Tees

The Diary Of Violet Storm

Monday 8th November

It rained today. The sky was really black (to match my mood). I was late for school because I *had* to walk. I got soaking. Well at least I had my personal CD player and my Green Day CDs with me. My favourite is 'Kerplunk'. I sang really loudly all the way to school. People were staring at me as if I were mad. I probably am. I'm weird too, that's what everyone says, but I don't care, I think it's cool to be unique and not follow the crowd.

Tuesday 9th November

Everyone was laughing at me today because this girl in my class called Claire thought it'd be funny to trip me up, so I was lying flat on my face, my books everywhere. Then my bag broke so I had to carry everything round with me all day. Then I got a football kicked at my face. I just wanted to scream, 'Why don't I ever get good luck?'

Wednesday 10th November

I take it back, I take it all back, I do get good luck, I do. Oh I'm so happy, I want to dance and shout. I can't believe it, me, Violet Storm, the most unpopular girl in Y8, got picked out of hundreds of people to go on tour with Green Day. Oh my God, I don't believe it. I danced all the way to school. I was so happy.

Monday 15th November

Meeting Green Day I nearly fainted. At exactly 9am they came, Green Day came to my house. They arrived in this wonderful green limo and this posh guy in a top hat escorted me into the limo. And there they were - Billie, Mike and Tré - and they were like so nice, talking to me like I was a real person and it felt so good.

When we arrived at the concert hall where Green Day were doing a small gig, it was like wow! I was all done up in green and black, cool! When Green Day came on I screamed and cheered until I couldn't anymore. Just before they played my favourite song, '2,000 Light Years Away', Billie said, 'I'd like to dedicate this song to Violet Storm. Gosh, she's so cool and pretty, this is for you Violet!' And that's when I fainted.

Louisa Thornhill (13)
Our Lady & St Bede RC School, Stockton-on-Tees

The Big Race

One Monday afternoon me and my friend went to town to the joke shop. In the window there was a notice for the big race. We went to my friend Callum's to make plans for our car.

We went to a scrapyard to get our bits and pieces. We got four pieces of 50 by 50 wood, 4 wheels off a pram, a car seat and a steering wheel.

We went back to Callum's into his garage. My friend John went to get some superglue. We put it together. It was a beauty. We were finally ready for the big race.

It was the big day. Our dads dropped us off.

'On your marks … get set … go!'

We were off. Two lads, Darren and Dazo, they were miles ahead but on the last corner their wheels fell off.

Yeees! We had won with the Automobile!

We went to Callum's to celebrate. We had won, yes!

Jamie Murphy (13)
Our Lady & St Bede RC School, Stockton-on-Tees

A Day In The Life Of Robbie My Dog

Robbie is my dog and he is very lazy and the only time he gets out of his bed is when he needs a wee or to see the dogs next door.

On a Monday morning I take him out for a wee and he runs straight out to the fence and looks for the dogs next door. Robbie sometimes is sad when they are not there, but when they are he starts to sulk. Then after half an hour he finally comes in and starts to eat his food. He then jumps up the stairs and climbs back into his bed and goes back to sleep.

In the afternoon he goes for a ride in the car with my mam and dad to the park or the beach, depending on the weather.

If it is raining he will have a day's rest in his bed or watch TV with me and my mam.

At night he comes walking into my bedroom and he sits looking at me so I stroke him. When I do this he jumps up onto my bed and he comes and licks my face then goes to the bottom of my bed. Sometimes he comes under the covers and goes to sleep with me.

Andrew Teasdale (13)
Our Lady & St Bede RC School, Stockton-on-Tees

A Day In The Life Of A Shoe

As the shoe lay across the bedroom floor it remembered being shiny and new in a shop window. Now it was scuffed and glued down at the front.

The shoe wondered why every day it got tortured in the same way - a girl would force her fat foot into the shoe stretching it outwards and then a brush would be scrubbed across it, and it would be slapped against the cold floor all day. The shoe wished one day it could go back to the shop.

One day the shoe got pushed into a black hole. The following day the shoe was tipped into a metal container that smelt like rotten eggs. It got taken to a warm room. From there it was melted and recycled back into a shoe.

The shoe got its wish to go back to the shop.

Elizabeth Harrison (13)
Our Lady & St Bede RC School, Stockton-on-Tees

This Is My Day!

The sun has risen and I have woken. Oh yes it's a beautiful day. The birds and the bees fly around in the fresh air. I pull myself out of my bed and go to get dressed into my ugly school clothes. Then I go downstairs to eat my breakfast - a lovely bacon sandwich, mmm. I stroll out of the front door after giving Mum and Dad a big, sloppy kiss. Ooh I do love them.

I am on my way to school when I meet my friend Ross and we continue our journey to school.

School slowly creeps by and I return back home. My tea is made for me as I walk through the door. I go on the computer for a bit then move swiftly onto my PlayStation. I go to bed when the time reaches 11pm, then when I wake up, the day starts again.

Joe Powell (13)
Our Lady & St Bede RC School, Stockton-on-Tees

The Old House

I walked up the old, long, winding path. The trees had taken over and had weeds climbing up every trunk.

It looked as if no one had been there for hundreds of years. All of a sudden there was a flash of lightning and a crash of thunder. The rain poured down.

I ran until I came to the old house. I opened the door and stepped in. The door slammed shut behind me.

I walked up to the passage and opened a door. It led to the lounge. Cobwebs hung everywhere. A huge spider crawled down my back. I screamed and ran out of the room. I ran upstairs and into the bathroom. Bats flew out of the airing cupboard and up to the loft. I started to climb up to follow them. I looked up and froze …

Bethany Sexton (13)
Our Lady & St Bede RC School, Stockton-on-Tees

A Day In The Life Of Me

This is how my day goes.

I wake up all tired and don't want to do anything. I slowly get out of bed and walk down the stairs. I watch TV and have my breakfast. Then I get ready for school. I walk out the door, get into the car and set off for school.

I get to school and see all my friends, that brightens up my day, seeing them all happy, laughing and jumping about. That's just what makes me happy.

The bell goes, time for lessons, boring lessons. I can't wait till breaktime to have a laugh.

Then it's time to go home. I say bye to my friends feeling upset but tired and want to go home to my bed. I get home, get changed and go out with people that live round mine. I don't get to go out with my friends from school because I live further away from them. However, I get to see them at the weekend, which is great.

Christina Alessi (13)
Our Lady & St Bede RC School, Stockton-on-Tees

A Day In The Life Of Captain Foley

1944 - a dismal year. The 6th June, Operation Overlord began. First, with the guys landing on the beaches, then me and my team landing behind enemy lines. When my feet touched the ground I noticed that my team were not with me because of a miss-drop. I freed the area around me. I just did not know. Fortunately I found a couple of guys from three other companies - Fox, Dog and Easy Company. They were aware of the miss-drop. We stuck together.

Luckily for us, Private Elder had a map. We found out where we were, only kilometres from St Mere-Eglise. We started pushing through, knocking off a few Jerries on the way.

Soon we came across a corporal from Easy Company who had been shot, probably from a soldier in the nearby bunker. Luckily he dropped his leg bag without it being picked up by the Jerries. The leg bag contained vital radio equipment to call in the main force to the drop off point. I just hoped that the AA guns did not pick them off first. The Germans that were in the nearby bunker were easy pickings and did not stand a chance.

We advanced into the field and radioed the paratroopers, advising our co-ordinates. Soon after we watched them all from the sky and land safely.

Sergeant Moody was part of the team, so we advanced to St Mere-Eglise …

Jordan Rollings (13)
St Aidan's County High School, Carlisle

A Day In The Life Of A Grass Lawn

As I lay there sunbathing on the ground and the gentle breeze blew through my long green blades of grass, I thought of how much I loved summer. As I looked up I was over watched by a white-petalled daisy, then as it looked down I remembered its familiar yellow face.

'Hello Daisie!' I yelled.

'Oh hello Grass, I didn't see you there!' she replied.

Daisie was usually very happy but today she seemed worried and tired. 'What's the matter?' I asked.

'Oh … erm … erm … I have been awake all night waiting for the … the … erm … the evil one, the lawn mower!'

'Oh no, not the lawn mower!' I said as I snuck back into the crowd of sleeping grass, looking round nervously.

'Yes, it's going to come and cut us one by one,' she whispered.

'Argh!' A scream came from the never-ending green blades surrounding me.

Suddenly a bulging feeling built up inside of me as if I was going to be sick.

'The evil one, argh!'

'Daisie, what's happening?' I screamed almost too quick, she couldn't hear it.

'Oh no,' she replied in a quiet, shocked whisper. She stood there with her petals blowing around and her small mouth wide enough to actually fit the lawn mower in.

A big orange motor came flying over the green landing a few metres away from Grass and Daisie, its gigantic engine pumping, sending black fumes into the air. As it came nearer it stopped, suddenly. It had no petrol!

Chris O'Carroll (13)
St Aidan's County High School, Carlisle

A Day In The Life Of A Slave

My name is Yakin and I am a slave working on a white man's plantation in Washington.

I am 14 years old and I have a child aged 3 months. The baby's father is the plantation owner and to make me pregnant he raped me and now he has disowned my child.

I live in a mud and straw hut on the outskirts of the plantation. My job is to play with the plantation owner's daughter called Mary. Even though I am not meant to be able to read or write, Mary has taught me to do such activities.

I live in my hut with my mother, my son and my newly found boyfriend Tommy, who was taken from Africa like me. My father sadly died on the way over to America, he jumped off the ship because he was so distraught.

I am now hoping that one day everyone will rebel against the plantation owner and there will be no more slaves imported to America.

I heard yesterday that slaves were now free in England and I am hoping soon slaves will have freedom in America. I can't wait for the day I am free and I can take my mother, Tommy and my son back to Africa where we belong.

I am very glad that we are able to go to the trees at night and pray for freedom, with the other slaves, to God because my religion is so strong.

I again say that I can't wait to be free. *Please think of me!*

Simon Brockbank (13)
St Aidan's County High School, Carlisle

A Day In The Life Of Jack Tyler

On Friday the 13th of October Jack Tyler and his friend were in Manchester Airport going to Tenerife. Jack went into a small shop and when he came out Ryan wasn't there. Jack went back into the shop to check if he was in there but he wasn't. Jack started to panic as he didn't know where Ryan was, or what had happened to him. Jack checked the time, he had less than an hour to find Ryan or he would miss the flight.

Jack had checked everywhere - toilets, pub, cafés, reception, restaurants, but he couldn't find him anywhere. He went to find the help and information centre to ask the hostess if anybody had been looking for him and if she could ask if Ryan Jones could come to the help centre.

The hostess had said that the speakers were broken but Ryan had been to look for a Jack Tyler. Jack calmed down as he knew he was safe and somewhere near the desk, and he'd just missed Ryan. Jack checked his watch - ten minutes till they had to board the plane. Then Jack spotted Ryan sitting on a bench. He ran to the bench shouting at Ryan. Ryan turned around looking relieved.

With 5 minutes left they both ran to Terminal 3. They both just made the flight to Tenerife.

Siobhan Waters (13)
St Aidan's County High School, Carlisle

A Day In The Life Of A Runaway Child

The day began early for Laura. She was used to the early mornings. Laura had run away from home and was living on the streets. She had met other children who had run away from home. Every morning she would go to the newsagents and ask if there was anything she could do to earn enough money for a meal. Sometimes there would be small jobs she could do to earn some money.

Afterwards she would meet up with some of the other kids that had run away. She had failed to get any money today so she couldn't afford anything to eat. She hadn't had anything to eat for three weeks. She had lost a lot of weight and was always ill.

That night it was one of the coldest nights since Laura had run away. She was becoming seriously ill. Then a policeman came walking along the streets and had spotted Laura and the rest of the kids. He walked over to them and looked at Laura. He could tell there was something wrong. He gave her his jacket and then phoned for an ambulance. Laura got put into the ambulance and another car arrived and all the other kids jumped in. Laura was taken to hospital.

A social worker came to see her and a few weeks later she was back with her parents. She was glad, even though she had run away. She still kept in touch with the other kids who were in the children's home.

Stacey Fraser (13)
St Aidan's County High School, Carlisle

All In The Day Of Hanna Brown

'Argh!' Mam cried as the car rammed into the car in front. I was crying, absolutely terrified. I didn't know what was happening. I can remember thinking I was dead and that shortly an angel would take me up to Heaven.

Mam just lay there with blood all over her face where the glass had showered onto her. There was a faint heartbeat. I frantically searched for her mobile but I couldn't see it for the tears running down my face. She must have left it somewhere. I needed to act fast, Mam needed help that I couldn't give her. She needed an ambulance.

I leapt out of the car and ran down the road. There were only dimly lit street lamps on either side of the road but they didn't do much. I ran further and further down the road and when I looked round to see the mangled car it was only a small dot in the distance. Hooray, I'd found something, a telephone box, just what I needed, so I dialled 999.

'Police, fire or ambulance?' said the voice.

'Err … ambulance please,' I said, catching my breath.

'Can you tell me what's wrong?' asked the croaky voice.

'My mam's had a bad car accident and is just breathing.'

'Okay,' said the voice, 'an ambulance will be on its way now!'

I sprinted back down the dark street, all the way praying that Mam was going to be OK. I saw the blue flashing as the ambulance crew took care of her. After that everything went blurry. I just remember meeting my dad at the hospital with my sister Holly, and my dad saying, 'Everything is going to be OK.'

Debbie Nixon (13)
St Aidan's County High School, Carlisle

A Day In The Life Of Dan

Dan, Liam and Calum have been friends since secondary school. They do a lot of things together.

One day Liam phoned Dan to ask him to go to a garage to buy his new car, a Porsche Carrera, so Dan agreed to go because he wanted to see Liam's brand new car.

Dan drove down to the garage with Liam in the passenger seat.

'So are you excited?' asked Dan.

'Yeah, I can't wait to drive it home,' he answered enthusiastically.

'So, are we going out later on for a drive?' asked Dan.

'Yeah if you want, you can drive if you like,' offered Liam.

'Yeah I'd love too,' answered Dan.

Dan pulled into the garage and Liam got out.

20 minutes later a fantastic blue Porsche drove out of the garage. It was Liam's brand new car.

Dan followed Liam home, then quickly jumped into Liam's car and drove away.

Dan was going quite fast down a country road when suddenly out of nowhere a rock came flying at the car. Noticing this, Dan swerved and drove into a signpost doing 70mph.

Dan jumped out of the car and ran to the front of the car. 'Oh no, I've wrecked Liam's brand new car.' Panicking and worried, Dan got his mobile out and phoned Calum and begged him to go out and meet him.

Calum arrived at the crash and just stared in disbelief.

'Calum, thank God you're here, I've ruined Liam's new car and I need to get it fixed now!' he shouted in a panic.

'How?' questioned Calum.

'There's no time for that, you have to swear you won't tell Liam.'

Calum and Dan took the car and booked it in to get it fixed. Meanwhile, Calum was with Liam and accidentally told him what Dan had done to his car. Liam was in a complete rage and phoned Dan screaming about his car. Dan was trying to explain but at the same time telling Calum that he hated him.

So Dan went to the garage and paid them for fixing the car. He took it back to Liam and begged for his forgiveness.

'I'll only forgive you if you make up with Calum,' said Liam.

'OK, I'll forgive him,' answered Dan.

'Right, you're forgiven, but you're never driving my car again!' joked Liam.

Ryan Charlton (13)
St Aidan's County High School, Carlisle

A Day In The Life Of …

'Why's Carlos moving in anyway?' screamed Lilia.

'Because he's my boyfriend. I love him Lilia. Can't you accept that?' shouted Madison.

'He's a stupid freak. I'm just looking out for you,' Lilia ranted, with tears streaming down her face.

'If you're not happy for me, I can't be your mate.'

'Fine.'

Carlos was upstairs, unpacking his things, listening to the girls quarrel, and came across a shiny lamp in one of his cardboard boxes. He thought, *I haven't seen this before. Is it mine?* But then suddenly a bright blue genie swooped out of it, and started talking.

'I'm Zucoflick the genie and I'm here to grant you one wish, but in turn you have to do something for me.'

'I know what I'll wish for, I'll do anything for Lil and Mads to shut up,' Carlos muttered.

'Well you said anything … '

There was a poof and Carlos was surrounded by genies. He had turned into Zucoflick and, without warning, the king genie approached him and announced, 'Zucoflick, it is your turn to be assessed.'

Carlos was handed a list of requirements for the assessment.

'If you don't complete the tasks, you'll be executed. Get on with it!'

Before Carlos had time to read the list, the real Zucoflick appeared.

'I've granted your wish, you can go home.'

'That wasn't long.'

'Yeah well, you got your wish, so it doesn't matter.'

Carlos was returned, and came home to a house full of peace and harmony.

What has just happened?

Kelly Ashbridge (13)
St Aidan's County High School, Carlisle

A Day In The Life Of A Garden Chair

It all started well for me today as Mrs Kennedy came out with her newspaper and cup of tea and had a nice lounge on me. She kept shuffling around though. My wooden frame was about to crumble. The sunny morning was turning into a dull grey afternoon and soon enough it was raining - heavier and heavier. It soon turned into hailstones and the wind made such a racket.

Oh no, here we go, I thought. The guttering at my end of the house was overflowing. And sure enough out came Mr Kennedy to try and unblock it. With the hard rain, noisy wind and an 18 stone man on top of you, it's hard to keep steady. All of a sudden I felt uneasy. Something was wrong, I knew it. Mr Kennedy knew it too. He took a deep, long stare at my base, so rude he is! He expected me to keep steady while his great fat lump was on top of me.

My legs were breaking, the strain was tremendous. I couldn't cope much longer. I could see Mr Kennedy was nearly done. The water from the gutter came down hard, along with leaves and other bits and bobs. It made a terrible mess, and I got covered. Finally the pressure had gone. He stepped down slowly and pushed me back to where I came from.

Garden chairs can be useful in lots of ways, remember we are human ...

Beth Johnston (13)
St Aidan's County High School, Carlisle

A Day In The Life Of Raji

Raji is a drug addict so he doesn't have much money. He does whatever he needs to for drugs. One day he was desperate for drugs and money. He had huge eyes the size of the bottom of a coffee mug. He had foot-long dreadlocks. He had black skin and was fairly tall.

Raji was walking down the street when he spotted a woman walking in front of him. This woman was Michelle Brown. She was on her way to work at the post office. Michelle noticed Raji following her so she crossed the road. She turned round and Raji had gone. She looked forward and Raji came sprinting up the road, his dreadlocks drifting through the wind and his huge eyes glistening in the early morning sun. He grabbed the woman and threw her in a bush. He hit her again and again until she didn't move. He ran off with her handbag and took her make-up but left her money.

Michelle woke up in hospital. She had a fractured skull and severe bruising. Her eye was the size of a tennis ball. Raji has not been caught but don't worry, Crimewatch is on the case.

Adam Brannan (13)
St Aidan's County High School, Carlisle

A Day In The Life Of Jak The Dragon

It was sunrise in the magic kingdom of Keru and the chirping of the bluebirds woke me up. I'm Jak and I live on the outskirts of the castle as a guard. I raised my head off the oak log and yawned, then I saw the servant of the king coming up to me. He was a green dragon with large wings.

'Jak, you have to wake up, the king wants to see you,' he yelled, then he walked into the castle. I followed.

The great hall was large with flames flickering at the side.

'Ah the guard, we have promoted you to be the dungeon's guard. If you don't get in there by 7pm you will be locked up. Now go!' ordered the golden king as he pointed to the big doors.

I arrived at the dungeons and tried to open the door. I got electrocuted. It was magically sealed and I needed magic to open it. Luckily I got my grampa Magi to fly over to the dungeon and teach me magic to open the door. I rolled a ball of fire and broke the seal to the dungeon. I thanked Grampa and flew to my room where I rested my head on the pillow and fell asleep.

In my dream I was fighting off evil with my new magic powers then I was promoted by the king to a heroic warrior. I woke up and decided to live my dream.

Thomas Brown (13)
St Aidan's County High School, Carlisle

The Favela Storm

I could hear the storm rising up over the dykes from the sea. At first it was a slow rumble, but as the storm got closer to land, the clouds started to gather, the sky darkened and the slow rumble became a very deep, dark groan.

It started to rain. I could hear it pound against the roof and hit the windows with such force that it cracked them. I could see trees and grass being swept up into the storm. I ran to my bed and hid under the covers fully dressed.

Outside I could faintly hear screams of pain and horror as the Favela people's houses were torn apart and destroyed. Their few possessions swept up away with one gust of wind as their corrugated iron houses collapsed.

The rain turned to hail. The hailstones seemed to be large because I heard one of the downstair's windows smash.

Suddenly I felt the house being ripped up out of the ground. My bed started to slide and hit the walls of my room. I was thrown from my bed, screaming. My baby brother started to cry from a distance and I realised that only the upstairs of my house had been ripped up. For the first time in my life, I was alone.

Christina Errington (13)
Teesside High School, Stockton-on-Tees

The Pensioner's Tale

(In the style of 'The Canterbury Tales' by Chaucer)

There was once an elderly gent, very distinguished, who was a cunning businessman and a favourite amongst the ladies. He owned a successful local pub which served a fabulous Sunday roast drowned in gravy. This man was Niall Nesbitt, a landlord respected for his age, quick wit and the ability to outrun anybody in his village.

The tale began one fine summer's day. The villagers had gathered for a fun-filled afternoon in 'Nesbitt's', and were crammed in to buy their drinks. As the wine was flowing and dancing had begun, a group of rowdy youths barged into the bar, knocking Millie Simons head first into the punch bowl. Niall was furious but he decided to let it lie and clean up blubbering Millie.

Soon the group of lank-haired boys began to make a nuisance of themselves, so Niall, who was as old as those four boys put together, asked them politely to leave. Of course, youths being youths, they refused. Niall thought on his feet, as he often did, and challenged one boy to a game of darts to decide who would leave.

The young lad accepted confidently as his friends jeered at Niall, who they thought had no chance. As the match began tension filled the air. Each competitor stepped up, three darts in hand. For a short while it was a close game - that was of course until Niall began to try. It was a white-wash and the boys had to leave in shame.

'Come back soon,' called Niall bellowing with laughter and contentment.

The bar was peaceful once again, and the elders drank heartily well into the night swapping tales from their lengthy and interesting lives.

Lauren Sinden (14)
The English Martyrs School & Sixth Form College, Hartlepool

The Banker

(In the style of 'The Canterbury Tales' by Chaucer)

Character introduction for the Banker

There lived a man who came from York,
Greedy, grasping and liked to talk.
And if in conversation cash,
Was mentioned he'd be like a flash,
To talk of profits, loans and rents,
Savings, funds and investments.
He'd talk and talk and talk and bore,
His bright teeth shining in his jaw.
Money was his only passion,
He hadn't any sense of fashion.
He was stout and stingy, liked to eat,
Had a baldy head and clumsy feet.

This is his story:

There once was a man who was deeply in love with a beautiful young woman. She agreed to marry him - but wanted the biggest and most spectacular wedding ever. In order to make this celebration possible, he had to borrow money from a wealthier friend. The friend refused. It was a large sum and he knew the man would struggle to pay it back. The man felt desperate, so he decided to offer his wife to the friend, should he not pay back the loan in two years. The friend agreed.

The wedding surpassed everyone's high expectations and the couple lived happily together. The man quickly forgot about the payment he owed and started to gamble and drink.

Two years had nearly passed and he remembered his promise to pay back the money or give up his beautiful wife. Desperately, he tried to sell and auction his possessions, but he was too proud and attached to some of the more valuable ones and couldn't raise the money.

After exactly seven hundred and thirty days from the time of the agreement, his friend visited and forcefully demanded the cash. The poor man, unable to pay up, could only watch with disgust as the sleazy 'friend' walked away with the love of his life.

Joe Harrison (14)
The English Martyrs School & Sixth Form College, Hartlepool

The Advisor

(In the style of 'The Canterbury Tales' by Chaucer)

This is a story of very ancient times. In those days people used to be very superstitious and had blind-faith in priests.

Once upon a time, in the thick dark forest, there lived a small family that consisted of only three people. Father, Mother and daughter who lived peacefully in a haunted place. They were more than happy with all that God had given them. They were self-sufficient and never asked for more. But, in this life, along with some happiness, there comes sadness.

One day, while the little girl was playing around the house, there came a poisonous animal. It was a snake. The girl was too innocent and too small to understand anything. Before the girl realised danger, the snake bit her. The girl dropped dead on the spot.

Soon her mother went searching for her and found the dead body of her poor child. The mother was absolutely shocked and horrified. She could not believe her eyes. Desperately and hopefully, she took the dead body of her daughter to a priest.

After hearing the sad mother's story, the priest first calmed her down. He told her, 'On this spot I promise you to bring this innocent child back to life only if you can give me grains of rice from a house. These grains should not be from a house where anyone has yet died.'

At first the mother thought that this was an easy job and she excitedly ran towards the houses of the people asking for rice grains. Everyone was ready to give the grains but when she asked about the death in their family, she could not find a single house where no one had yet died. By evening she sadly came back to the priest.

The priest explained to her that death is a part of life. Everyone has to accept the death of their loved ones sooner or later in life, and still life goes on.

Anuj Vakharia (14)
The English Martyrs School & Sixth Form College, Hartlepool

The Knight

(In the style of 'The Canterbury Tales' by Chaucer)

One day a young nobleman was riding along on his horse with the king. Suddenly he had a thought. If he killed the king, maybe the new king would make him a knight. He decided he would, after all, why not? He pulled his sword out and with one stroke, cut the king's head off.

The next day the king's body was found by a knight. The knight was outraged and carried the king's body home. In the next few days the country was disgraced. The king had been murdered and no one had a clue as to who had done it.

The king's funeral was held and afterwards a new king was appointed - King James IV. This king was a ruthless man and swore revenge on whoever had killed the old king. Eventually the young nobleman was found out and was arrested. The king said he had 6 months to live. He was imprisoned in the highest tower.

Now, while he was living the last 6 months, he fell in love with the queen. The queen, who was only young, was married to the king, who was very old. When this young nobleman came along she fell in love with him. Every night she went to his prison cell.

On the day he was about to be beheaded, she said her last goodbye and vowed one day she would be with him again.

As he put his head onto the block, praying to God for his forgiveness, he heard a shout. He looked up and it was the queen saying, 'I love you and always will!' For this she too was beheaded by his side.

So they were together again, in death.

Tim Snowdon (14)
The English Martyrs School & Sixth Form College, Hartlepool

A Day In The Life Of Jack Higgins

My favourite place is my mate's end - it is rundown and full of drug dealers but you can play footy, 'De-la-la', 'Block', bikes, climb walls and the kids can fling cans, bottles and mud at you.

There are two main places for footy - the road (which is never used) or the field. We never play there either or alternatively, Dyke House Astroturf. The road looks like a rundown, abandoned street with a yellow fence (goals) that has planks missing but it has big, heavy green, steel graffitied doors that are securely padlocked shut.

Over the road is an old house with a fence up to your hips but there is a tall bush to stop us getting over. It has a large garden and beside it is a garage and driveway. My friend climbs onto the roof sometimes when playing 'De-la-la' and 'Block'.

There are many streets and driveways to hide in. The second pitch, the field, is a big-sized body of grass with a lamp post and bin making goalposts on one side; and a huge cream wall on the other, beside the grass and the road no one uses, and a big kerb.

Jack Higgins (12)
The English Martyrs School & Sixth Form College, Hartlepool

The Hunk

(In the style of 'The Canterbury Tales' by Chaucer)

There was a hunk, a handsome lad, who had a fiancée, Isabella was her name, a fine girl she was.

One glorious day, the hunk decided that he wanted Isabella to be his wife. As they walked the promenade, the hunk proposed and she said yes with no hesitation.

Sadly, all was not well, as his mother, Mrs Highland, a mean old hag, was against the idea of her son being married to, what she thought, was a devious woman.

As they wined and dined, and their spirits were high, his mother secretly planned to have his wife murdered. When, you may ask. It was to be the wedding day, when all was happy. However, instead of a wedding, it would be a funeral.

Whilst the hunk and the bride were getting dressed in separate houses, Mrs Highland stayed with Isabella keeping a close vigil on her. As the time came near, the mother and bride dressed in their best and left the house with the mother behind the bride. The mother then pulled out a knife and stabbed the bride until she was dead.

Anxiously waiting, the hunk realised something was wrong and went to see his wife-to-be at home. As he arrived he heard sirens. He knew something had happened. Standing there he noticed his wife being placed into a body bag.

His mother stood there covered in blood. However, she did not leave the house because he stabbed her, just as she had done with his bride, and he's been on the run since.

Natalie O'Boyle (13)
The English Martyrs School & Sixth Form College, Hartlepool

The Judge's Tale

(In the style of 'The Canterbury Tales' by Chaucer)

At the foot of Mount Rilargo, Spain, lay a tiny fishing village. Crimes committed here were taken very seriously and the villagers themselves decided the punishments.

In the village lived two sisters. The sisters seemed like twins. They had the same proportions, same flowing chestnut locks. Their faces, however, were a different story. Sascha had a sweet pretty face with carefully placed freckles. She was loved and adored by all. Bridget had a large, dominating nose and wide-set eyes. She was nothing special to the villagers. Bridget was extremely jealous of Sascha but she disguised her feelings. She craved the love and attention. Bridget began to steal. She thought that if the villagers' attention was on the crimes, then somehow the attention would be on her.

At first Bridget stole things that she did not believe mattered to the people. Of course the village was in uproar.

One late Friday night, Bridget decided to steal something she had never stolen before - money. She crept out and snuck inside the village hall where the money was kept. Just as she grabbed the money box, she heard shouts behind her. She kicked up her heels and ran as fast as she could home. It seemed she had lost her pursuers in the chase.

The next morning the whole village came and pounded on Sascha and Bridget's door. It seemed as if someone had seen a thief - the thief with the long flowing chestnut hair. Without a moment's hesitation, Bridget pointed to Sascha. The villagers suddenly seized Sascha and hauled her off to the desolate tower. Out of love for her sister, Sascha let them take her. Sascha remained there for many years until one day the villagers took pity on her and freed her.

Samantha Mason Port (13)
The English Martyrs School & Sixth Form College, Hartlepool

Forbidden Love

(In the style of 'The Canterbury Tales' by Chaucer)

There was once a maid called Sarah. She was made to do the foulest jobs imaginable by her master, Lord Hereford. To add insult to this she was only paid two pennies a week for all her work.

Her life was miserable, but no matter how bad it got she couldn't quit because her family had worked for her master for generations. Getting another job would be impossible.

Her life did improve though when her master hired a new driver. He was called Michael and he had the cutest blue eyes imaginable. His short blond hair was adorable and Sarah soon fell in love with him.

Michael had also fallen in love with Sarah. He loved her long brown hair, her beautiful, slim waist and her cherry-red lips. But most of all he loved her fantastic green eyes.

They were both madly in love and started a secret romance together. Unfortunately, their love was so strong, their master discovered the truth.

He was furious. He wanted them both hung for insolence, but luckily his wife managed to persuade him to just sack Michael, and let Sarah continue to work in the castle.

Lord Hereford agreed to the plan and the day for the separation came. It broke the lovers' hearts and a tearful goodbye was the last time they saw each other.

To this day they still have not been reunited.

Charlotte Carney (13)
The English Martyrs School & Sixth Form College, Hartlepool

The Fisherman's Story

(In the style of 'The Canterbury Tales' by Chaucer)

It was a normal day and I was out doing a bit of sea fishing. The water was pretty calm, with just a few waves. The sky was blue and free from clouds.

I had just caught my first fish of the day when the sky suddenly seemed to cloud over. The sea turned a murky grey colour and the winds began to pick up.

The waves grew larger and larger, and they started to rock my little boat. I decided to head back towards the shore, and started to turn her around. That's when it hit.

A wave as big as twenty houses hit my little boat. It pitched me out and then carried the boat back to shore, throwing her into some rocks. She was smashed into splinters.

Meanwhile, I was struggling with the waves out at sea. I'm not the best swimmer. I didn't really try to learn because I thought that I would be spending most of my time in the boat, not in the water. I think I may have blacked out because I don't remember anything else from that day.

The doctors said I was lucky as all I got from that day was this scar. It could have been a lot worse, I suppose.

Rosie Timlin (13)
The English Martyrs School & Sixth Form College, Hartlepool